The elevator stopped and the doors opened, startling her again. For one second, she had forgotten what had sent her rushing into Reve's building.

She had to quell a compulsion to hurry into the belly of the penthouse in search of him the way she used to, calling his name. Oh, what she wouldn't give to throw herself at him and feel his strong arms close around her. To let him kiss the hell out of her and take her to bed before barely three words had passed between them. The outside world had always ceased to matter when they were lost in passion.

But that was all in the past. And much as she would love to hide from reality, she had learned that it eventually had to be confronted.

"Nina." He appeared abruptly, the mere sound of his voice awakening her blood.

The Secret Sisters

When their paths cross, expect explosions!

World-renowned model Oriel Cuvier and
esteemed fashion designer Nina Menendez are
complete strangers. But unbeknownst to them,
they share a shocking secret that, once revealed,
will shake their worlds to their core!

And the similarities don't end there because
everything is set to get even more complicated
with the arrival of two commanding men who set
their hearts racing and their skin on fire! Will they
both succumb to the temptation...?

Read Oriel's story in
Married for One Reason Only

And discover Nina's story in
Manhattan's Most Scandalous Reunion

Both available now!

Escape into the scandalous world of Dani Collins's
sexy and irresistible duet The Secret Sisters.

Dani Collins

———

MANHATTAN'S MOST SCANDALOUS REUNION

HARLEQUIN®

PRESENTS®

Recycling programs
for this product may
not exist in your area.

ISBN-13: 978-1-335-56799-4

Manhattan's Most Scandalous Reunion

Copyright © 2021 by Dani Collins

This edition published by arrangement with Harlequin Books S.A.

For questions and comments about the quality of this book,
please contact us at CustomerService@Harlequin.com.

Harlequin Enterprises ULC
22 Adelaide St. West, 40th Floor
Toronto, Ontario M5H 4E3, Canada
www.Harlequin.com

Printed in U.S.A.

Canadian **Dani Collins** knew in high school that she wanted to write romance for a living. Twenty-five years later, after marrying her high school sweetheart, having two kids with him, working at several generic office jobs and submitting countless manuscripts, she got The Call. Her first Harlequin novel won the Reviewers' Choice Award for Best First in Series from *RT Book Reviews*. She now works in her own office, writing romance.

Books by Dani Collins

Harlequin Presents

A Hidden Heir to Redeem Him
Confessions of an Italian Marriage
Innocent in the Sheikh's Palace
What the Greek's Wife Needs
Her Impossible Baby Bombshell

Once Upon a Temptation

Beauty and Her One-Night Baby

Signed, Sealed...Seduced

Ways to Ruin a Royal Reputation

The Secret Sisters

Married for One Reason Only

Visit the Author Profile page
at Harlequin.com for more titles.

To Doug, who graciously accepts the burden of being married to a writer. I love you.

CHAPTER ONE

NINA MENENDEZ WAS having a garbage day on top of a painful month in what was starting to look like a horrendous year. She'd didn't need a pesky man with a camera getting in her face, accusing her of being someone she wasn't.

"Oriel! Hey, Oriel."

Especially not that woman.

Nina's heart lurched in one direction while she veered in another, trying to hurry away from the Manhattan hotel where she'd tanked an interview with a British film star in town for a talk show. Nina didn't even want to go into costume design. Did she? She didn't know anymore. She didn't know who she was or what she wanted. Everything was wrong in her world. She might as well go to the garden and eat worms.

If she only *had* a garden. At the rate she was going, worms were all she could afford.

"Oriel. Why are you here? Where is your husband?" The photographer skipped alongside her, maniacally snapping his camera in her face.

Paparazzi hung around the entrance to swanky hotels like that hoping to ambush the celebrities who stayed there. In her case, she'd been trying to get on with an indie project that the star was producing for herself in London. It wasn't a big budget, and Nina had only been granted an appointment thanks to a friend pulling strings, but she'd said all the wrong things and was beating herself up over what felt like self-sabotage.

"Are you working again?"

Well, that was just mean, wasn't it? She almost used her subway language, but kept walking, ignoring him.

The photographer kept after her and some of his colleagues did, too. They nipped like hyenas with baiting questions as they tried to get her attention.

"Why aren't you in India?"

"Is it true you're pregnant?"

"Look." She had to stop at the corner to wait for a car to turn in front of her. "I know who Oriel Cuvier is, but I've never met her. I just happen to look a little bit like her." Freakishly very much like her, but Nina was trying really hard not to think about that.

Being accosted and mistaken *as* her wasn't helping. Why had she thought coming back to New York was a good idea? Oh, right, to find out *why* she looked so much like a stranger.

"Who are you then?" one demanded, following her into the next block.

"Nobody. Go home and compare our photos."

That's what Nina had done after a friend from

work—back when she had *had* a job—had remarked on how much she resembled the French model. That had been eons ago, when Nina had arrived in New York for the first time, bright-eyed and full of dreams. The photo of Oriel Cuvier on a runway had been making the rounds in fashion circles for the professionally tattered and much-lauded gown she had been modeling.

Nina had found their similarities unnerving, but other events had soon consumed her.

Now, after licking her wounds in Albuquerque for three months, she'd scrambled to get back here for that stupid interview, and it was the worst possible timing.

Oriel's star had already been rising, but Nina had nursed vague hopes of crossing paths with her. As she had arrived, however, Oriel had slipped out of the city, emerging in India, where she promptly began to dominate international headlines.

Oriel Cuvier was the previously unknown daughter of a Bollywood screen queen, and photographers were positively rabid to catch a photo of her.

"Her hair is different," Nina pointed out, mostly to shut them up. Thanks to Nina's sister's love of tints, Nina had streaks of pinkish red in her otherwise very similar near-black hair. Of course, the streaks were hidden by the half bun she wore. She'd been trying to look professional for her job interview. Maybe that had been her mistake. Maybe they had wanted someone with flair.

Maybe she should quit worrying what others

thought of her and be herself. Who was she, though? Ignoring the twist of anxiety that went through her, she kept talking.

"Her mouth is different, too." The model's wealthy parents had been able to afford braces. Nina had a slight overbite. Hopefully, the photographers wouldn't look beyond that, because the shape of their full lips matched perfectly.

"Her profile says she's five-eleven. I'm five-nine." And three-quarters. Basically five-ten. Today, however, she was so dispirited she was probably five-three. "I'm not her."

"Who are you then? Talk to us. Are you related to her?"

"Why are you still bothering me?" She walked faster, annoyed, and also growing alarmed. She was a twenty-five-year-old woman being swarmed by a half-dozen men. The bustling people they passed averted their gazes, signaling they didn't want to get involved.

"Tell us why you're not in India. Oriel!" One of the men grabbed her arm.

Nina's self-defense training kicked in. She spun and jammed the heel of her palm into his nose.

The impact reverberated from her wrist to her elbow, all the way to her shoulder. A jarring rush of adrenaline poured through her chest like fire. She bounced back on light feet while her bag fell off her shoulder and swayed on her arm, knocking against her knee.

The man swore and bent, blood from his nose

painting the sidewalk in bright blotches. The rest of the men fanned out, jeering and swinging their camera lenses between the injured man, who was straightening with a look of retribution in his eyes, and whatever terror was written into Nina's expression.

Dear God, they were everywhere. She was surrounded. Her airway tightened and her wild gaze swerved every direction, seeking a path of escape.

A blue-and-silver awning struck her eyes. She had walked in this direction unconsciously on purpose because, deep down, she was a masochist.

Normally, she would have stayed on this side of the street and glared upward as she walked by, but in her agitation, she darted straight for the entrance, not computing that she was running into traffic.

A car squealed its brakes and stopped on a dime right before it would have struck her. The driver laid on the horn, then honked again as the horde of cameramen chased her, all of them batting and bumping into the car in their haste to get around it.

Nina brushed past the startled doorman and ran inside, straight to the security desk where Amir sat today.

"I'm sorry. Please, can I stand here a few minutes while I figure out what to do? They won't leave me alone."

She was quivering with reaction, breathless and barely able to speak. She looked back to see the doorman holding out his arms while he ordered the men, "Back off! No entry."

Amir frowned at her, then at the disruption outside. One of the men evaded the doorman and pressed his camera lens to the window, clicking and flashing through the glass.

Amir picked up his phone and dialed.

Was he calling the police? Nina's scrambled brain tried to decide whether she should involve them.

"It's Amir, sir. Ms. Menendez is here in the lobby."

"What?" she whispered. "I didn't come here to see *him*."

Her stomach began to churn. She held her breath in dread-filled anticipation.

"Yes, I understand, sir. But she seems upset."

Her heart stalled out. How humiliating. After seducing her and leading her on, Reve had dumped her when she had asked if he wanted to meet her father. Three months later, he didn't even want to see her.

She covered her face, turning her back to the windows so she had a shred of privacy while she tried to think of where she could go or who she might call. The few friends she'd made in New York had fallen away when she'd been fired and moved in with Reve. And the friend who'd gotten her today's interview lived in London. The one who was loaning her his studio was backpacking in Australia.

She didn't know what to do. She was upset by more than the fact those men had chased her. It was everything that had happened lately. Her ears were rushing with the sound of her galloping pulse. Her life was falling apart at the seams, but she couldn't crawl home this time. Where *was* home? *Who was she?*

"Miss…" Amir's voice was loud enough to make her jerk her head up. His frown told her he'd had to repeat himself to get her attention. She saw he had opened the doors for Reve's private elevator.

"Mr. Weston will see you. Would you like me to come with you? You seem unsteady."

She stared into the elevator, longing to see Reve even though she knew he only pretended to rescue damsels. Deep down, he was more of a dragon who lured them in and ate them.

Still, she could hear the doorman arguing with the men outside. She had to leave the lobby so they would disperse. She desperately needed to be transported out of her entire overturned, mixed-up life, and, God knows, Reve's world was the furthest thing from her own.

Her feet moved her into the elevator, and she instantly flashed back to what seemed like a million years ago but was really only three months ago. She had felt on top of the world then. Staying in a penthouse apartment overlooking Central Park had a way of doing that to a person.

She had stood right here every day, convinced she was in love and barreling toward happily-ever-after. Rather than work for someone else, she had begun to sew her own collection. She had anticipated that, by the end of summer, she would have enough for her own show at fashion week. Just a small thing that was more like a gallery showing, but it would gain her exposure, help her network and maybe glean her a few orders from boutiques. She'd flounced about in her own creations, each one set off with handbags and shoes and bangles that Reve had paid for.

She'd left it all when she'd walked out, sickened that she had let him buy her for the price of soutache and organza, Microtex needles and glass-headed pins.

Oh, how the mighty had fallen. Today she wore a simple maxi-dress she'd made from fabrics leftover from her college days. The knot of hair behind her crown had begun to fray while her natural waves had picked up the summer humidity, and flyaway strands were sticking to her face and shoulders.

She had hoped this look would project that she was casually chic, approachable and open to collaboration. Unfortunately, her portfolio said she hadn't worked since last year and never in costume design. She wasn't going anywhere and had nowhere else to go.

Being so self-pitying wasn't her usual MO, but even her reflection had ceased to feel like it was hers. Not when another woman had claim to it. Not when defeat dragged at the corners of her mouth and her eyes were hollow from weeks of sleepless nights. The dusting of makeup she'd put on this morning stood out starkly on a complexion that was a pallid version of her natural golden tan.

The elevator stopped and the doors opened, startling her again.

For one second, she had forgotten what had sent her rushing into Reve's building. She had to quell a compulsion to hurry into the belly of the penthouse in search of him the way she used to, calling his name.

Oh, what she wouldn't give to throw herself into him and feel his strong arms close around her. To let him kiss the hell out of her and take her to bed before barely three words had passed between them. The outside world had always ceased to matter when they were lost in passion.

That was all in the past. And as much as she would love to hide from reality, she had learned that it eventually had to be confronted.

She stepped tentatively into the foyer with its gold-veined marble and a round table holding a floral arrangement that was replaced every three days.

"Nina." He appeared abruptly from the hallway to the bedrooms.

The mere sound of his voice awakened her blood. The sight of him fed a thirst she had vainly tried to ignore since she had left.

He wore crisp, dark gray trousers and his feet were bare. He was shrugging on a blue-and-white-striped shirt over his muscled chest and flat abs. There was a faint glow beneath his winter-in-Florida tan and a sheen upon it. His dark hair was damp and messy.

Even amid her confusion of shock and fear and dread, she was taken aback by how ruggedly handsome he was. The uncontrollable attraction she'd felt from her first glimpse of him burst to life inside her, starved for that hint of curl in his dark brown hair, his steely blue eyes, his square jaw and his impervious air of assurance.

It felt so good to see him again that a smile began to tingle in her cheeks and pull at her mouth before a painful realization struck like a jagged spear of lightning, cleaving her apart and leaving her soul nothing but an acrid whiff of its former self.

"You're with someone." She knew how he looked when he was climbing out of bed after lovemaking. *Like this.*

Her knees went weak. She was so nauseated by despair, she lowered herself onto the upholstered bench by the elevator and leaned forward, trying to keep herself from fainting.

This was what a mental breakdown felt like. In her head, she had known he would move on. Confronting it like this was the final straw, though. She was flattened. Destroyed. She couldn't face him. She had to go, but her legs refused to work.

"I'm alone," Reve said in a clipped voice. "I was showering after my workout when Amir called. But I am on my way out."

That sounded like a warning. *Don't get comfortable.*

She lifted her head and, despite the standoffish wall that seemed to form a barrier between them, his gaze searched hers. Maybe, if she hadn't been at the very end of her rope, she might have thought there was a wary tension deep inside that look.

"Why are you here?" He scanned her thoroughly from her disheveled hair to her open-toed sandals, and whatever he saw made his brows slam together, thunderstruck. "Are you pregnant?"

"What?" She sat up so fast she bumped her head

on the wall behind her and had to rub the hurt away. "*No. Gawd*, that's all I would need right now."

Only a complete fool would mourn the fact she had no lifetime reminder of her gullibility in getting involved with him. Then she must be a fool, because not being accidentally pregnant by him had made her very blue.

"Why do you think I'm pregnant?" Her dress was loose because it was midday and the hottest June on record, but she hadn't gained any weight. She was one of those annoying people with a high metabolism and had been told her whole life she could be a model or a basketball player. The second one had always been discounted about five seconds after she fumbled the ball and chased it, kicking it away in the process.

"You look like you're going to faint. Are you ill?" He had instantly gone deep inside himself in the infuriating way he had, becoming impossible to read.

"I'm fine." She really wasn't.

"Then why are you here? For your things?" He looked to each of his cuffs as he buttoned them, all business. "I texted to ask what you wanted me to do with it."

She had blocked him. She had feared if she started talking to him, she would fall right back under his spell. Which she was in danger of doing right now. *Help me, Reve. Save me. Love me.*

"This was a mistake—" She rose abruptly, and the blood rushed from her head. She set a hand on the wall as she swayed dizzily.

Reve quickly stepped forward to catch at her.

She just as quickly pulled away, brushing his hands off her. She was pretty sure she would dissolve into tears if he touched her. In her haste, she staggered into the bench, dislodging it and causing its feet to screech on the marble.

It was classic clumsy, reflexive Nina, but her panicked reaction had shocked him. She saw his eyes flash with outraged astonishment, then a shadow of stunned hurt.

He quickly blinked it away and took a few steps back, holding up his hands.

"You're totally safe here, Nina." Now his voice was grave and reassuring and nonthreatening enough to make her all wobbly inside.

She was acting hysterical. She *was* hysterical. It was taking everything for her to hold back the tears swelling in her throat.

"I just need somewhere to collect my thoughts," she mumbled, feeling foolish and messy and horribly gauche. Was this why he hadn't wanted a future with her? Her whole family found her disorganized and overly sensitive and somewhat oblivious.

It was true. She often didn't have a single clue despite what might be staring her in the face. She led with her heart and saw only what she wanted to see. That's how she'd missed the fact she wasn't actually related to any of her relations. That's how she'd mistaken a wealthy man's desire for a mistress as love at first sight.

"Do you want to come sit down?" He waved toward the living room.

She moved into the familiar space of his penthouse with its vaulted ceiling and wall of windows looking onto the terrace. As she sank into her favorite corner of the overstuffed sectional, the one that faced the fireplace, she pulled the cushion from behind her back and hugged it.

"Would you like something? Coffee? Tea? A drink?" He was keeping his distance, which made her feel again like she was being melodramatic.

It was his influence making her act this way, she wanted to say. When she was with him, he sharpened her reactions to everything. The sun shone brighter, food tasted better. Orgasms became otherworldly.

"No," she murmured, biting her lip to distract herself from how much she had missed him.

It's okay to love someone who doesn't return your feelings, her sister had said when Nina had crawled home, a failure on all fronts. *You still got to feel it. Love is never wasted.*

Easy for her to say, married to her high school sweetheart and still deeply in love.

"Do you want me to call the police?" Reve's carefully neutral tone was unnerving. He was an assertive man who always knew what he wanted. When he had an opinion, he voiced it. If he thought a certain action should be taken, he took it.

Treating her as though she was made of spun sugar was making her unravel even faster.

"I haven't been attacked," she mumbled.

"There's blood on your bag. And your hand."

His voice wasn't quite steady. His shoulders were a tense line.

She realized he was boiling with rage beneath that clenched jaw. She looked to the floor where she'd dropped her shoulder bag. One of the sagging ropes that formed the handle held a streak of red. The heel of her palm also had blood on it.

Wonderful. Now she had to scrounge up the energy to go to the powder room.

"I shouldn't have barged in on you like this." She rubbed her thumb on the stain. "I was at a job interview a few blocks over. Paparazzi chased me when I came out of the hotel. One grabbed me and I punched him in the nose."

"Because you and I were involved?" Reve's frown was instantly thunderous. He hated sensational publicity. *Hated* it.

He picked up his phone, not waiting for her to clarify before he spoke to someone she presumed was Amir. "Get the names of the men outside. Let them know charges of assault will be forthcoming." He ended the call.

"Against me?" she asked with a thin laugh. "*I* hit *him*."

"Good." He moved to the wet bar and soaked a cloth under the tap. "We've all wanted to do it."

"*Not* good. I feel awful about it."

He gave the cloth a hard twist to wring it out and brought it to her. "We're all entitled to defend ourselves. I guess those classes your sister dragged you to paid off."

He remembered her telling him that? She'd mentioned it the first time he'd offered to drive her home so she wouldn't have to take the subway. The classes had been the only way her sister would allow her to leave for New York alone.

"Thank you." Nina accepted the cloth and wiped her hands clean. "But it wasn't about you."

How strange to acknowledge that when her life had been revolving around him from the moment she had met him on New Year's Eve. She'd been at the party as an assistant to her former employer, Kelly Bex, one of New York's top designers. Kelly had wanted to snare Reve's attention for herself, not that Nina had realized it. Seriously, she was *so* clueless.

"Be nice to him," Kelly had said. So Nina had made a point of introducing herself, saying something that had made him laugh. She hadn't realized he was a self-made bazillionaire who had gotten his start selling used car parts and was now a driving force—pun intended—in autonomous vehicles.

They'd chatted for a half hour and, rather than going home with Kelly, Reve had taken Nina's number, asking her to dinner the next evening. Nina had mentioned it to Kelly at work the next day, innocent as a spring lamb, asking if there was anything Kelly wanted Nina to bring up with him.

While Reve had seduced Nina that night, Kelly had browsed recipes for cooking and eating the hearts of her enemies. It wasn't until Nina was holding a cardboard box of her things on the street a few days later that she'd realized she'd been fired in direct retaliation for her budding affair with Reve. Her roommate at the time had also been an employee of Kelly's, so Nina had lost her sublet, too.

Reve was a much faster study. He'd understood the dynamic straight away but hadn't been particularly remorseful. However, since Nina had had no job and no home, he'd taken her in and offered to make reparations by supporting her career aspirations. She had let him act like a superhero because she had thought he believed in her work and wanted her to succeed.

He had wanted her in his bed. That was all. That was the happily-never-after to that story.

Even after she'd figured it out and tried to move on, he had affected her life. He'd left her so hollowed out she'd abandoned her dreams and scurried back to Albuquerque, where she had struggled to even look for work. She had lived with her father and swept hair in her sister's salon. When she did go on interviews, she failed to land jobs because she was walking around with such an angry look on her face.

Not today, though. Weirdly, this thing with Oriel Cuvier wasn't about him. At least, it hadn't been until she had run in here and drawn him into it.

Oh, heck. He was going to kill her when he realized that.

Reve took the cloth and threw it all the way across the room, where it landed in the sink with a dull thud.

"Why are they chasing you, then?" He dropped into the armchair that faced her. "Some other man you're seeing?"

She could have barked out a wild laugh at that.

What did he think? That she had walked out on him for turning her into a paid escort so she could take up with another man in exactly the same capacity? As if she could even think about other men after him. Even as she sat here, she was thinking, *Why couldn't you have loved me just a little?*

She gave herself a mental shake and said facetiously, "Yes. Duke Rhodes." Oriel Cuvier had been at a premiere in Cannes with the actor six weeks ago. That's what had started Nina down this rocky path of self-discovery. "Haven't you seen our photos?"

"The has-been from those 'Frantic and Fuming' action movies?" He grimaced. "He's too old for you."

"I'm being sarcastic," she said with exasperation. "You really haven't seen them?"

"You blocked me, Nina," he said in a tone that was falsely pleasant. "How could I see any of the photos you post?"

Wasn't it supposed to feel satisfying when the object of your block realized it? She just felt petty and obvious. Now he knew how much he'd hurt her.

"They're not my photos. They're on the entertainment sites."

"I don't look at that garbage." His face hardened with genuine anger. "But if they're chasing you because of him, why the hell would you lead those vultures to *me*?"

CHAPTER TWO

"I DIDN'T! I was across the street and they surrounded me. I panicked and ran to what was familiar." She hugged the pillow she was still holding. "I didn't expect Amir to call you." Her chin trembled. "I just wanted to catch my breath."

Reve had been born skeptical. The life he'd led had honed his cynicism to a razor-sharp edge. The first time Nina had spoken to him, he'd seen her angle. She'd been cutting in line ahead of her own employer, a shark of a woman named Kelly Bex, to get to him.

That put Nina on his own level of ruthless buccaneering—not devoid of a conscience, but willing to leap on an opportunity when it presented itself in a bespoke suit with a Patek Philippe wristwatch and a gold credit card made from actual gold.

He respected that. Plus, she was pretty as hell. Mesmerizing with her silky, shiny hair and her expressive brows and her delicate oval face. She was curious and interesting and made him laugh, so he'd let her run her game. Why not? He liked to play as hard as worked.

He'd thought he was embarking on an affair with a like-minded partner, but their relationship hadn't gone the way he'd expected. Nina possessed an artistic temperament. She was naturally passionate and sensitive and effusive. She challenged his assumptions, and pushed up against him and *excited* him. Sparks had constantly been flying, especially in the bedroom. They were an A-hazard combustible combination, and his body refused to forget it.

The lust she provoked in him had been her ticket into this penthouse. He'd known he was being a fool. Emotions were a tool for manipulating a reaction. He sat in marketing meetings all the time where they discussed how to stir up envy and turn it into a luxury car purchase, but he'd still allowed her to enthrall him.

When she had stormed out because he had declined to eat dinner with her father, he'd seen it as a tantrum intended to bring him to heel. He'd balked—hard—expecting her to come back once she cooled off, but she hadn't.

Her social feeds had reassured him she was alive and spending time with her father, and then three days later he'd seen a "good to be home" post. The phone he'd bought her turned up at the desk downstairs, and he discovered she had blocked him from every aspect of her life.

That abrupt cutting of ties had thrust him into a fractured moment of fearing he had genuinely hurt her. Dread had leaned a sharp elbow into his integrity.

He wasn't the most moral of men, but he didn't *harm* people. He didn't use them up and throw them away.

He didn't need them, either, but he felt her absence more keenly than he'd expected. It still put a sick knot in his gut recalling how discarded he'd felt for those few dark minutes.

Then he'd remembered that she'd left her precious sewing machine. This whole charade was a taunt. She had wanted him to chase her, but he refused. He'd sat back and waited, knowing she would turn up when she was ready, and here she was.

The part where she was claiming to have been chased here by paparazzi was an odd way to save face. Definitely *not* the quickest way into his good graces, but he knew how nightmarish those scrums could be and she seemed genuinely distressed. There was a haunted look around her eyes. Tension pulled at the corners of her mouth. Her cheekbones stood out as though she'd lost a few pounds. She was naturally slender and tall, but she had never struck him as fragile.

His heart sat crooked in his chest as he realized she hadn't smiled once yet. In fact, she looked like a rabbit run to ground.

"Are you sure they didn't hurt you?" he asked with gruff concern.

He was still twitching with adrenaline from noticing the blood on her hand. For a few seconds, he'd gone to a very violent place. He'd always been a scrapper, but today, imagining someone had hurt her so badly she was terrified of him, he had known he could kill.

It was sobering. And a stark reminder that she brought more tumult into his life than was comfortable. In fact, he was sitting here filtering through a thousand reactions when he ought to have already dismissed her from his life and left for his engagement.

"I'm fine." She was rubbing her thumb into the heel of her palm. "I might have a bruise later, but I'm just…" She heaved a sigh that contained a metric ton of despair. "Tired."

That he believed. The way she stared sightlessly at the fireplace, her mouth pouty with desolation, bothered him. He didn't like seeing her like this, trampled and sad. It slipped past the armor he was donning and sank like an ice pick in his gut.

He fought softening toward her while she blinked slowly once, twice, then drew a breath and shot him a tight, brave, flat-lipped stretch of her lips that was evidently supposed to be a smile. She set aside the pillow.

"You're right. I shouldn't have come to you."

His lungs tightened in a very visceral reaction. Why not him?

This was her strange power over him, though. She said and did things that tugged reactions from him with a barbed hook. He didn't want to be the sort of man who could be led by his emotions. It left him open to all sorts of strikes.

He clenched his jaw against any declarations of concern or offers to help and stood.

She rose and shouldered her bag, tugging her hair

free from the strap, making him want to reacquaint himself with how satin-cool those wavy tendrils were and how warm and smooth her skin was.

He jerked his gaze away. "I'll take you out through the underground parking and drop you wherever you're staying." It was the decent thing to do. That was the only reason he offered.

"A subway station is fine, thanks."

"I'll take you home," he insisted. "Your things are in storage downstairs. It will only take a minute to have them load—"

"No." She hit him with a look that accused him of hate crimes. "Why do you still have it? Sell it. Give it away. Throw it away. I don't care, but it's not mine." She disappeared into the powder room and slammed the door.

And there was the flare of temper that lit his own, making him want to bang on the door and demand she explain herself.

No. He wouldn't let her manipulate him again.

He went down the hall to finish dressing, determined to end their association once and for all. Determined to ignore the gravel that sat heavy in his stomach as he did.

"Do you need a few more minutes?" Reve asked stiffly as she joined him in the elevator. He'd put on a tie and jacket and looked fantastic, the bastard.

Nina looked and felt like the crumpled tissues in her hand. She was as tired of crying as she was of everything else, but why had he thrown her shattered dreams in her face like that? Why?

"I'm fine." She felt his gaze on the side of her face, intense enough to leave a radiation burn.

His car was waiting by the elevator when it opened. He moved to open the back door himself and she slid in, slouching down even though the windows were tinted.

He came in beside her and gave her a disgruntled look, then flicked his gaze to their surroundings as though checking for cameramen.

"Where are you staying?" he asked.

"Lower East Side."

"Where?"

"A friend's studio. His lease runs out at the end of the month and he's in Australia. He said I could use it. The price was right." She spoke with indifference, as though she wasn't dreading going back there. "Drop me at whichever subway station is along the way," she told the driver, adding to Reve, "I don't want to keep you from…whoever you're seeing."

She flicked her gaze to his razor-sharp lapels, trying not to contemplate who he'd dressed to see.

"It's a lobbying fundraiser," he said.

"Oh, well, you know I'd love nothing better than to keep you from giving crooked politicians your money. Take me home, then," she said facetiously.

"Sorry to disappoint, but I've already paid for the tickets. Lower East Side," Reve said to the driver, and closed the privacy screen.

"I was being sarcastic. The subway is fine."

He put up a finger as he dialed his phone and brought it to his ear.

She looked out the window. The word *tickets*—plural—had stuck like a blade in her stomach. The knife twisted as she heard a woman's voice answer his call.

"I'm running late," Reve said. "I'll meet you there."

Nina did her best to transport herself out of body while the woman promised to "tell Daddy" and said, "See you soon."

"Dating a politician's daughter is not the way to stay out of the spotlight," she remarked pithily when he ended his call.

"It's cocktails on the lawn. I don't *make* the rules, you know. I simply play them to my advantage."

"Sounds like you're playing *her*." She used the voice of experience.

"She called me to say that if I bought the very overpriced tickets, she would join me to make introductions." He dropped his phone into the inside pocket of his jacket. "That's how the system works, and that's how I have a chance to swing things into better practices than the ones you hate. I recently succeeded in getting emissions regulations tightened, so you're welcome. Breathe easier."

"Don't act like that was about the planet. You're only trying to make the field more even for your hydrogen fuel cells."

"Air quality still wins."

True. And she wasn't swiping at him for chasing

political influence. She was jealous. That was the ugly bottom line.

They drove several blocks in silence, the commuter traffic heavy but not awful.

"Why are *you* in the spotlight?" he asked in a tone shaded with skepticism. "You never said."

"It's a long and b—" She'd started to say *boring*, but it was tragic and painful and confusing and life changing. Potentially more so, if she pursued it, but she didn't think she had a choice. Not if she was being chased through the streets demanding answers she didn't have.

She dug into her bag, found her phone and then pulled up the photo of Oriel from Cannes.

Reve gave her screen the quickest, most cursory glance. His mouth twisted with faint disgust. "So you *are* seeing him."

"Read the caption."

He took her phone and stared longer. Frowned. "Oriel Cuvier?" He flicked his gaze to her face and back to the photo. "That's you."

"Nope." She reached for the phone. "She's a French model. Runway work, but also underwear and swimsuit ads. She recently landed one of the top brands for sunglasses. When I first came to New York, someone pointed out a photo of her and said we looked alike. I didn't think much of it. We all look like someone, right?"

"Your dad was in the air force, wasn't he?"

"Funny you should mention that, but don't malign the fidelity of a man you refused to meet. Especially because if you had, you would know he's white. What are the chances he would have two daughters with such dark coloring? If you say he must have a type, I will poke you in the eye."

He held up a placating hand. "What's *your* theory then?"

She looked at the phone, loathe to go to that other image because it made her seriously question her sanity. Her stomach had been nothing but acid since she'd seen it. She gathered herself and flicked, then handed her phone across, not glancing at the two photos that had been juxtaposed by the press in India. They showed a mother and daughter, both in their midtwenties.

"That's why Oriel Cuvier is making headlines right now," Nina said to the window. "She was adopted by a French couple and raised in France, but she recently learned her birth mother was Lakshmi Dalal, a Bollywood star who died about twenty years ago."

Reve scrolled to read the article beneath.

Nina dug into her bag for the keys to the building so she wouldn't have to look at him. Was he thinking she was pitiful? Reaching for a connection that was laughably beyond her? Soft in the head?

He didn't swear or give any indication of his reaction.

When she dared glance in his direction, he was watching her.

"Are *you* adopted?"

"No." Her throat closed, making the word more of a squeak. The pressure in her chest became nearly unbearable. Her eyes grew so hot she had to clench them to prevent the tears from leaking out.

"So this is a coincidence?" he scoffed. "A quirk of genetics?"

"Must be." She snatched back her phone, so abruptly it bordered on rude, and threw it into her bag. "Now all these stupid reporters think I'm her. I'll have to go back to Albuquerque so they'll leave me alone except I *can't*." She leaned to rap on the glass and then pushed the button to lower the screen. "Make a right at the light, please. I'm eight blocks up, but let me off wherever you can."

"I'm not letting you off here." Reve glowered as they rolled into a street full of stained awnings over pawnshops and moneylenders. There were homeless people sprawled with their belongings on the sidewalk. A woman in a short skirt paced alongside their slowing car and leaned suggestively, trying to catch Reve's attention.

"It's daylight. I'll be fine. I'm in the middle of the next block," she told the driver, pointing at a very dodgy building that had half its windows boarded up.

Reve swore and curtly ordered the driver, "Let us out here and drive around the block." He turned back to her and added, "I'll walk you in."

"Why?"

He ignored her and stepped out of the car after her, taking hold of her elbow as they crossed the street and walked the remaining block. He sent alert glances in both directions and subtly placed himself between her and the man blocking the entrance to the building.

"Spare change?" the man asked.

Reve handed him a few dollars, and his grip tightened on Nina's elbow as they moved into the darkened entranceway at the top of the steps.

"Why the hell are you staying in a place like this?" The simmering rage was back in his tone.

"I told you. It was free." She tried the key, but the building's front door had been broken in since she'd left this morning. It swung inward as she touched it.

"You're smarter than this, Nina."

"It's not that bad," she lied, secretly relieved that he was following her up the two flights of stairs. She unlocked the door to the studio and they entered what was admittedly a dim, squalid room of peeling paint and hard-used furniture. "See? Perfectly fine."

"Why is the window nailed shut?"

"My friend was robbed a few weeks ago, but it's safe now, right? No one can get in."

"It's a firetrap," he said grimly. "Get your things. You're not staying here."

"It's for a couple of nights. It's *fine*."

"There's a full bag of garbage right here." He pointed. "You know that attracts rats, right?"

"That's actually my suitcase. I bagged it to keep the cockroaches out."

He gave her the most condescending look in the history of condescending looks.

"So you're already packed," he said with muted fury. "Good."

"I'm not staying with you," she insisted.

"Well, you're not staying here, so tell me which hotel you want to go to."

"It's been so nice seeing you again, Reve. I can't imagine why I told you to go to hell and walked out on you."

"Yeah, I'm awash in warm fuzzies myself. Do you have more than this?"

"I don't have money for a hotel! And don't you dare tell me you'll pay for it. I already owe you thousands, and I feel sick about it every single day. So no, Reve. *No*."

"What are you talking about?" he muttered crisply. "I have never expected—" His phone pinged. "That's probably my driver telling me he's losing the hubcaps." He glanced at his phone and his expression turned to concrete. Accusation flashed into his eyes.

She fell back a step. "What?"

"My publicist is texting," he said through his teeth. "Asking if I want to make a statement about my relationship with Oriel Cuvier, since she was seen coming into my building. There's speculation we're involved. So, yes, Nina. You will come home with me. You are going to tell me *exactly* what is going on, and we're going to find a way to keep my name out of it."

CHAPTER THREE

REVE DIDN'T BOTHER unknotting the garbage bag. He tore it open and left it on the floor, plucking her cheap red suitcase out of it.

"Get whatever houseplant you're supposed to keep alive and let's go." He was breathing through his mouth so the musty smell of this place wouldn't drag him into all of his worst memories.

Nina clenched her fists and tightened her mouth with stubbornness.

"I'm serious, Nina. I was used for publicity once before. *Once.* Never again. So you're coming with me and we're going to put a lid on this."

"Oh—" She whirled into the bathroom and came out with a yellow toiletry bag in one hand, a damp bra and underwear in her other. She shoved everything into her shoulder bag, picked up the romance novel off the coffee table and pulled a charger from the wall. She pulled a pink denim jacket off a hook and shrugged it on over her dress.

Minutes later they were back in the town car. Reve

texted his publicist that he would be in touch with a statement shortly.

Then he texted his "date," telling her he wouldn't make it. Nina was right: a politician's daughter was under way too much scrutiny for his tastes. He hadn't planned to take things beyond drinks, but he texted that he would have his people call her people, not so subtly relaying a message that he had no interest in a more intimate connection.

"Why involve me?" He clicked off his phone. "If you want to capitalize on this look-alike thing, that's your business. There was no reason to bring me into it."

She was slouched in her seat, hugging herself, face forward, chin set at a belligerent angle. "I told you what happened. If you don't want to believe me, that's your choice."

"You running back into my life the day reporters start harassing you is just a huge coincidence? That's what you want me to believe?" Did she think he was born yesterday?

Her hand was crushing her denim sleeve. She made a noise of annoyed defeat.

"Okay, I walked by your building on purpose. I wasn't planning to come in. I didn't even know whether you were home."

"Then why come by at all?"

"It's called closure, Reve. I was supposed to get the job I wanted. I was going to mentally flip you the bird and fly to London to get on with my life."

"How'd that go?" he asked facetiously, aware of a

gritty sensation in his middle as he imagined that plan playing out. He wouldn't have known she was right outside his door. It shouldn't bother him, but it did. "I didn't realize you were holding such a grudge. Is that what all of this is? Retribution for the way things ended between us?"

"What? No. Oh, my God." She sat up and glared at him. "I am sorry that your old girlfriend made a sex tape of you without your permission and posted it online. I didn't do that to you." She flopped back into her seat. "I would love it if you would stop blaming me for it."

"I don't," he growled, stung that she would even bring it up. The humility of it never went away, no matter how well his lawyer's takedown notices worked at keeping it from being shared. The exposure without consent was bad enough. The *you have nothing to be ashamed of* snickers turned the knife, but the worst was his own stupidity.

Reve closed his fist on his knee, hating that video for existing and hating himself even more for being gullible enough to think himself in love when it had been made.

"You don't trust me, Reve. You never have."

"I don't trust anyone," he shot back. "You're not special."

"Oh, I'm well aware of that," she said with a laugh that was a jagged scrape of sound. "She broke you. You're afraid to reveal a single thing about yourself that might be used against you. Here's news, though. We all get hurt. You're not special, either."

He drew in a breath that burned his nostrils.

This was something he couldn't stand about Nina. She had this way of turning things around on him, forcing him to self-examine. He hated it. He wasn't broken. He wasn't a psychopath. He was a law-abiding citizen who was considerate enough to let an old flame take refuge in his home. He'd walked her into that dive of an apartment and refused to let her stay there, hadn't he? He was capable of basic human compassion.

He wasn't *broken*.

"I take calculated risks, not stupid ones." That made him smart. His entire fortune was built on careful gambles. He made exactly as many bets as he expected would pay out. "So tell me what your game is and I'll decide if I'm willing to play."

"I'm not even good at games," Nina said with exasperation. "You're giving me way too much credit if you think I could put together some elaborate scheme against you. I can't win a hand of Go Fish against my niece. It's a family joke how obtuse I am. *All of this* is because of how slow I am to see the obvious." She turned her face to the window.

Her hand came up to her cheek, and he thought she might be wiping under her eye.

His heart twisted in his chest.

The car darkened as they came into the underground lot beneath his building. It stopped by the elevator and the driver came around to open Nina's door, then moved to the trunk to get her suitcase. Nina sat there unmoving, even when Reve came around to look at her through the open door.

"Are you going to be stubborn about this?"

"No. But I'm only coming up because I'm too exhausted to figure something else out. I haven't slept since I got here Sunday."

"Why not?"

"You saw the place. I was petrified."

He swore and held out a hand, helping her from the car.

She swayed slightly and he realized exactly how strung out she was. He wanted to draw her into himself, support her. Hell, he wanted to *hold* her.

Since when was he Mr. Affection? Since never. Touching during sex was great, but that's where cuddling and fondling belonged.

He made sure she was steady, then turned to punch in his code. The driver set her case inside the elevator and asked if there would be anything else.

"We'll have dinner from Antonio's," he decided.

"I'll cook," Nina said in a dull voice.

"You just told me you're tired."

"Would you *please* let me earn my keep this much at least?" Her tone shot up to a strident pitch.

"Fine," he muttered, and dismissed his driver.

They rode upward in thick silence.

He hadn't realized how often she had cooked until she was gone and he'd been stuck eating takeout again. Nina was damned good at throwing a meal together and had seemed to like doing it, but he'd always thought it was her way of playing house, pushing him toward domesticity and reliance on her. He wondered now if it had been her way of contributing.

I owe you thousands and feel sick about it every day...

A teetering sensation rocked behind his sternum. "You know I don't expect you to pay me back for—"

"Don't start that fight, Reve." The doors opened into his foyer and she shoved her suitcase out of the elevator. "I'll burn your dinner, and maybe the entire building to the ground."

Nina banged through the cupboards, taking a quick inventory and deciding she could manage some rice and peas and empanadillas.

She was tired, but there was something very soothing in making one of Abuela's standby dishes. It grounded her when she was otherwise completely adrift.

Reve appeared when she was wrist deep in dough. He had changed from his suit into tailored Bermuda shorts and a polo shirt. He looked casual, but tension radiated off him.

He had brought a bottle of red wine, which he opened, pouring two glasses and setting one within her reach.

"Thanks." She set the dough in the refrigerator and washed her hands before she sipped. It hadn't even breathed properly yet, but a small explosion of currants and black cherry and pepper hit her taste buds.

She had missed drinking wine that cost more than

a pair of shoelaces. She had missed a lot of things, especially this little ritual of theirs.

Reve lowered onto one of the stools at the island the way he often had when she'd cooked. Invariably, they would have already made love and were mellow and pleased to get a little loose over a bottle of wine, bantering and squabbling over the nonsense of everyday life.

Tonight, there was a cloud of animosity rolling off him. A sense that whatever she said would be weighed and measured and examined for signs of deception.

She moved to start the rice, saying, "I was born in Luxembourg. Did I ever tell you that?"

"That's a long way from Albuquerque." He screened his thoughts with his spiky lashes. "Close to Germany. Isn't there an airbase there?"

It was almost laughable how much quicker he was than she could ever hope to be.

She nodded. "Dad was stationed there and my m-mother—" This was the part that was really, really hard.

"Nina." He set down his glass, speaking in the quietest, most careful tone she'd ever heard him use. "If this is going places you don't want to go, you don't have to tell me."

"No, it's fine." She didn't want to imagine what he thought she was saying. "You're actually the only person I *can* tell. Maybe the best person, because you have no emotional investment. You're so cynical and blunt, you'll recommend a psych evaluation, which is probably what I need."

She turned away to get everything simmering on the gas flames and turned back to see him staring holes into her back.

"What?"

"Nothing." He blinked and whatever impression she'd had was gone. "Continue."

"This is how the story was always told to me." She began to chop peppers. "Our mother was feeling cooped up in the tiny flat they had near the base. She wanted to take my brother and sister to a cuckoo clock factory for a day trip, but they got lost. She accidentally crossed into Luxembourg and stopped at a café to ask for directions. She collapsed with an aneurysm."

He swore softly.

"Yeah." She flattened her lips. "The people in the café didn't know that's what happened, but she was super pregnant—a couple of weeks from being due. There was a private clinic nearby, one of those places for Europe's elite to dry out or get plastic surgery on the down-low. She was rushed there for treatment. My sister has this vivid memory of sitting in the café holding my brother's hand, terrified and confused. A man brought them cheese and crackers and hot chocolate. He asked where they were from. He was trying to find out how to get hold of Dad, I guess, because Dad showed up a while later. He took them to the clinic, where they got the bad news that Mom was gone. They were all crying until a nurse brought me out and put me in Dad's arms. Then they all stopped crying and smiled."

Nina had to take a drink to keep her throat from closing. Her chest was scoured with emotion, her eyes hot. "I've always felt loved because of that part of the story. Always."

A muscle in Reve's cheek twitched, and his gaze dropped into his glass.

He had never told her much about his childhood. He played his cards close to his chest, never spoke fondly of a brother or sister or a father or mother. He never, ever spoke about love.

"Your father didn't ask for blood samples or anything?" He was a man of facts and computation, and had a natural skepticism of any information presented to him. *He* would never take on faith that the baby placed in his arms was his own.

"Dad was completely distraught. We shipped home and Abuela moved in with us. Dad was absent a lot until he was discharged, but he was home permanently by the time I was going to school. I graduated, saved for college, got my degree, then came here to work." She shrugged. "It was all pretty normal."

"Until you learned there was a model who looked just like you."

"Yes, but then I met you and didn't think about much else." She tossed him a flat smile before she turned away to check everything on the stove. He had consumed her. Had he realized that?

"Do you believe you were sent home with the wrong family?" he asked quietly.

"No," she said without hesitation. "They are the most loving people in the world. I'm very lucky to have them." Her eyes welled, and she had to use the back of her wrist to clear her vision.

"You know what I mean."

"I do." She brought the dough from the fridge and floured the surface of the counter. "People used to ask me if I was adopted. It upset me, but Abuela said I took after her sister. She told me that was why I struggled in school, that it was a family thing to have dyslexia. She didn't use that word, but that's what she meant."

"I didn't know that about you."

"It doesn't matter." It did. It mattered a lot. It had impacted her self-esteem, but she had developed strategies to pass her assignments and graduate. Her fine arts degree majoring in fashion was one of her proudest achievements.

She had gone through life wondering why her brother and sister found basic things like reading and math so much easier than she did, though. It had set her apart from them, and now she felt like a complete idiot for not seeing she'd been different in a far more profound way.

"I never had any reason to question whether my family was related to me by blood, not until I offered to have my sister's baby."

He paused in reaching for the bottle to top up his glass. "What do you mean you 'offered to have'?"

"Carry it. As a surrogate." She found one of the wide-mouthed glasses she liked to use to cut circles in the dough.

"Why the hell would you do that?" His eyes flashed with astounded disbelief.

"She's my sister." It was all the reason she needed. "She and her husband have had fertility struggles for years. That's one of the reasons I went home. Dad told me over dinner that Angela had miscarried again. She was heartbroken."

"You never told me that about her."

"Because it's none of your business. I'm only telling you now because it's relevant." She filled a few pockets of dough and sealed them, then set them into the frying pan to begin cooking while she filled the rest.

"They've talked about using a surrogate on and off, but aside from the cost, it's a really personal thing. I offered once before, but I was still in college. Angela said it would be too disruptive to my education. She was so heartbroken this time, I was desperate to help. And I wanted to do something that would make me feel like my life had some sort of meaning or purpose."

"Nina." There was admonishment in his tone, but a man like him must know there was a huge difference between pursuing a goal and achieving it.

She crumpled up the scraps of dough and rolled it out again, leaning in hard.

"Surrogacy sounds simple, but it's a big undertaking. Most agencies won't let you do it until you've had a successful pregnancy of your own. Some people do it in private arrangements, and my doctor wasn't exactly encouraging about our doing that, but he was willing to at least screen me—"

"Blood tests," Reve said with dawning understanding.

"Yes. He sat me down with the results and said it wasn't uncommon for siblings to have different blood types, depending how your body puts your parents' chromosomes together, but I was enough of an outlier that he suggested I have a chat with my dad."

"Did you?"

"*No.* I told Angela I was anemic—which is true. I'm taking iron now." She gulped a mouthful of wine and turned the empanadillas in the pan. "Then I took one of those ancestry tests. I wanted to prove the doctor wrong."

"But?"

She released a shaky sigh. "My brother did one a few years ago when his wife didn't know what else to get him for Christmas. My results should have been in the same ballpark as his, right? If we both come from a Puerto Rican mom and a white American father? Marco's report said he was Spanish with some African and Taíno, which is the indigenous people in the Caribbean. Plus English and German, which lines up with where Dad's family is from."

"And yours?"

She felt a great pressure in her breastbone. "Some English. Mostly South Asian and Scandinavian."

"Scandinavian?" Reve snorted and searched her features as if looking for the evidence of Nordic blood.

She shrugged and emptied her glass in one gulp, then pushed it toward the bottle.

He refilled it. "Have you tried contacting the clinic?"

"The building has changed hands more than once. It's a spa resort now."

She checked the rice and turned it off, then prepared a couple of plates. She left a fresh batch of empanadillas frying in the pan as she took a stool next to Reve.

"The connection to Oriel wasn't on my radar when I got my results. I mean, there were photos of her with Duke Rhodes in the magazines at my sister's salon— What's wrong?"

Reve was staring at the plate she'd set in front of him.

"Nothing," he mumbled, seeming almost self-conscious. "It smells good." He shoveled a forkful of rice into his mouth and took a small breath around it because it was hot, but he didn't cool it with wine. He chewed and swallowed. "It's good. Thanks. Keep talking."

He proceeded to eat as though he hadn't been fed in a week.

She filtered her words carefully as she said them aloud for the first time.

"I wasn't thinking, *I wonder if she's my sister.* Not until her story broke about being Lakshmi's daughter. Then I read that she was born in Luxembourg the day before me. My time of birth is fourteen minutes after midnight."

He snapped a look at her. Then he finished chewing, swallowed and asked, "Have you reached out to her?"

"You're supposed to tell me I'm out of my mind, Reve!" She made herself eat because otherwise she'd have that bottle of wine for dinner. "You're supposed to say, *Save that imagination for the sewing room.* Say, *There's an obvious explanation*, then tell me what it is," she pleaded.

"It is obvious. She's your twin."

"Would you *stop*?"

CHAPTER FOUR

REVE CLEANED HIS plate in record time and rose to help himself to more even though he was already full. He turned the empanadillas over in the frying pan and then leaned on the counter, eating rice while he waited for them to finish browning.

God, this was good. He had never understood people who got nostalgic for certain foods. Eating was better than going hungry, so he ate what was put in front of him, but as the familiar aromas had gathered amid the sizzle and pop of the pan, a nameless tension inside him had eased. His mouth had watered.

Nina's story was not her usual animated discussion of buttons and weave and where hemline trends were headed, though. She looked miserable as she chased a pea and gathered a few grains of rice with the tines of her fork.

"This is why you were so upset when you got here," he realized. "It wasn't because the reporters were chasing you. It was because you couldn't outrun the truth."

She lifted her lashes and sent him a morose glare, soft mouth falling down at the corners.

"Suppose you are twins," he speculated. "Were you split up through incompetence or was it deliberate?"

"I came to New York with a half-baked plan to find out. I thought Oriel was here. Or that I would get that job—any job, but hopefully that one," she said with a curl of her lip. "I thought if I could get myself stationed in London, I could do some footwork from there. Take a train when I had time off, see if I could find someone who had worked at the clinic. I mean, I could send a few emails from here to… I don't know. The spa? Or see if I could find the doctor who delivered me. But if mistakes were made, no one is going to admit it. Not to someone whose life was changed because of it."

"They'll lawyer up and clam up."

"Exactly. If I go to Oriel, she's liable to do the same. Imagine how many people are coming to her with bogus claims right now, trying to get their hands on Lakshmi's fortune."

"Those people aren't wearing her face. You have an edge, Nina. One look at you and she will do a test to prove exactly what you already suspect."

"Then what?" she challenged with agitation. "Then I have to tell my family that the child they thought survived *didn't*. Is their baby out there somewhere? Living with strangers? I don't *know* Lakshmi gave birth to me, but if I go public with any of this I'll have to hire a bodyguard, because people will chase me down the street for the rest of my life."

She poked at her food again, head hanging over her plate.

He took out the cooked empanadillas and turned off the stove. "What are you going to do then?"

"I don't know. Tell me what to do because all the options I see are terrible."

"Tell your father," he said plainly, not bothering to cushion his words. "Prepare him for the fact that I'm going to tell people it was you, not Oriel, who came here today. Once he sees the photos, he's liable to have the same thoughts you do. You want to be ahead of that."

"Do I?"

"Why wouldn't you?"

The anguish and vulnerability in her expression made the hairs stand up on his arms. He unconsciously braced himself, expecting pain for some reason yet not understanding what kind or from where.

"What if he doesn't want me when he realizes I'm not his?" Her voice was so thin and vulnerable, it arrowed into his chest and left the space there cold and cavernous.

"Do you really think he wouldn't?" It was a stupid question. His own father hadn't cared if he'd lived or died.

"How would you react if you found out twenty-five years after the fact that you'd been raising a child who wasn't yours?" The anguish in her eyes was more than he could bear.

He had never planned to raise any children. If his own father was anything to go by, nurturing didn't come naturally to his kind, and so Reve had made the decision long ago not to perpetuate feral, junkyard hounds like himself or force anyone else's children to live with one.

Although, for those seconds in the foyer earlier, when it had struck him that she might be pregnant, his entire view had changed. For one flashing second, he'd seen a completely different future for himself, which had died a quick death when he heard, *That's all I would need.*

Obviously, Nina wouldn't be happy to be carrying his child, and why that left a hollow sensation in his chest was a mystery.

He brushed all of that out of his mind. Nina was begging for him to tell her that calling her dad would turn out fine. The brutal fact was that he was far too cynical to believe it. Based on what he knew of people, there was a very real chance her family could reject her.

And he instinctively knew that would break her. Whatever ulterior motives Nina might have where he was concerned, one thing had always been indisputable. She loved her family. She'd always had complete confidence that they loved her, and now that confidence was shaken.

She pushed her plate away abruptly and stood, her jaw set with decision, before turning toward the living room.

"Nina." He set down his plate and made sure everything was turned off before he followed her.

She was on the sofa with her phone in her shaking hand, instructing, "Text Dad. Do you have time for a call?"

There was a quaver of dread in her voice. Her phone whooshed and her anxious gaze came up to meet his.

Reve was ruled by logic. If you had a question, you asked it. If you had a goal, you found the quickest route to attain it and chased it until you got there. His head told him this was the right thing to do, but a hot lump formed behind his breastbone. What if he'd steered her straight off a cliff of some kind?

Her phone pinged and she gave a couple of quick voice commands.

How had he not noticed how often she used voice commands? He had, of course, but he hadn't understood the significance.

The robotic AI voice read aloud, "Dad. On a date. Will call when I'm home."

She slid her phone onto the coffee table and fell onto her side on the cushions, scowling hard enough a fire should have spontaneously burst forth in the hearth.

"Can you hold off for a few hours on making a statement?" she asked tersely. "I'll clean the kitchen in a few minutes. I just need to think."

"Of course." He went back to the kitchen long enough to put the leftovers into the refrigerator and fetch their wine.

When he set her glass on the coffee table, he saw she was asleep. The creases of tension had finally melted from her face, but dark circles were still smudged beneath her eyes. He wondered exactly how long she'd been living with all of these secrets and doubts, because that sort of exhaustion came from more than a few nights in a flophouse apartment.

When he realized he was staring and had his own brow pulled into a tense wrinkle of consternation, he drew a blanket from inside the ottoman and draped it over her.

Then he sat and picked up his tablet, calling up this twin of hers. He quickly landed on photos of Oriel in bikinis and sexy lingerie.

It was like seeing Nina in the bedroom and made him hot, but not in a titillating way. He was affronted on her behalf. This wasn't her, but it could be. This woman's figure was a little bit thinner—not much, but he knew Nina's curves intimately enough that the difference was obvious to him. Oriel had a polished gleam to her that contrasted with Nina's natural and very casual beauty, and Oriel posed in ways that accentuated her sexuality. Nina was far less overt.

These photos irritated him. Nina was modest at heart. She was passionate and sensual and uninhibited when she got into sex, but that was something she expressed in private. She wasn't one to flaunt excess cleavage, or flash her legs, or flirt and draw attention to herself.

The clear boundary around their sexual lives was one of the things he'd liked most about her. It was why he'd been comfortable letting her stay in his home. She didn't engage in shock talk or gossip about bedroom escapades.

Even so, from the moment she'd left, he'd been waiting for her to show her true colors, expecting her to exploit their relationship in some glaring tell-all fashion.

She hadn't.

Obviously, there was still time, but she wasn't racing to capitalize on the riches and notoriety of her likely association to Lakshmi and Oriel, either.

That left him with an uneasy suspicion he had pigeonholed her, failing to see past his own black-and-white judgments.

He absently played the backs of his fingers against the stubble under his chin as his mind strayed to the night she'd walked out, the move he'd convinced himself was purely a manipulation tactic on her part.

He never let himself replay their argument. When he recalled that night, he always stopped at the good part. They'd had sex when he got home after being away a couple of nights. Their lovemaking had turned into a hedonistic indulgence of their senses. He'd been drunk on her, kissing and suckling everywhere, caressing and licking at her most responsive flesh until she had been a quaking mass of lust.

She was incredible when she was like that, eyes glazed, lips swollen, body twisting without inhibition. Her voice got sexy as hell when she was that turned-on, and she knew it turned him on to hear it. She had told him what she wanted in the bluntest way, and he still got hard recalling it.

When she was aroused to that degree, he could unleash his own restraint. He'd slipped his arms under her legs so she'd been completely open to him. She'd reached to the headboard to brace herself, breasts jiggling under the power of his thrusts. The slap of their flesh and her animalistic moans had been raw and hot and wild.

Holding back to wait for her had been heaven and hell, but her tension had finally snapped in a rush of magnificent, glorious release. Her body had shuddered and her sheath had milked at his shaft. He had lost it. The orgasm that rocked him had been the most exquisitely sharp and sustained climax of his life. He still felt a dull ache thinking of it today.

Who remembered something like that? He'd probably had a hundred orgasms since, but he remembered vividly how hard he had come that evening—maybe because he replayed that evening nearly every time he was in the shower, he thought ironically.

He always stopped with that moment of culmination, though, not wanting to recollect the way she had wiggled his foot a millennium later, waking him from his sex-induced doze.

"I thought you would join me." She had worn only a towel. Her hair was in a clip, damp around her hairline, her face clean and fresh. "Are you going to shower before we go?"

"Where?" Maybe if he hadn't been drunk on endorphins and dopamine, he would have been thinking more clearly and handled things better, but his head had been full of cotton, his limbs made of lead.

"Dinner." She went into the closet and came out to throw a dress on the foot of the bed. "With my dad."

"Oh. No. I'm not going."

She had laughed, then realized he was serious and frowned with confusion. "I told you two weeks ago that he would be here to take me for a belated birthday celebration. That's why we waited until tonight, so you would be home and could come. You made the reservation."

"Yeah, they have my credit card. Go wild." He had curled his arm under his pillow, always happy to watch her move around wearing only a towel. "The car is yours, too."

"But—" She disappeared into the closet and came back wearing her bra and underwear. They were a lacy, spring green that made her skin glow like dark honey. "I don't understand. Did something come up?"

"No."

"Then why aren't you coming?" She leaned around the bathroom door to hang her towel. "Don't you want to meet him? He wants to meet you."

"I'm sure he does," he'd said drily. "But I know what meeting the family means and that's not where this relationship is going, so what's the point?" He had thought that went without saying.

Nina had come back into the bedroom to stare at him with a wide-eyed, ingenuous look. She was a master at this projection of artlessness. She'd worn the same look when she'd told him she had been fired, as though the news had arrived from left field.

He'd known from the outset that her boss was after him. He'd had no interest in the other woman and plenty in Nina. Since he was partially responsible for Nina's job loss and they were already sleeping together, he had said she could use his spare bedroom as a studio. He had no friends or family who came to visit so it was wasted space.

He had used those words when he offered it, so he couldn't understand how she might have read more into why he was letting her stay with him, but she'd stood there looking as though she'd been sucker punched.

"Where *is* this relationship going?" she had persisted. "Or not going, I should say."

He'd got his back up. Guilt had crept in—unwarranted. He didn't lead women on, but he had sensed her affront. In response, his own defense mechanisms had locked into place.

"Why does it have to go anywhere? We're both comfortable."

"*Are* we?" Her face had darkened and her hands had knotted into fists.

"Oh, I think you're very comfortable, Nina." He'd sat up to find his underwear and pulled them on. "Why are you acting like this? I told you on day one that I wouldn't let anyone manipulate me ever again."

"How am I manipulating you?" The doe eyes again, as though he was roaring down a country lane straight at her and she didn't understand what was happening.

"You're not. Because I'm not stupid enough to let you. I gave you what you wanted." He flicked a hand toward her studio down the hall. "That's more than I've given any other woman, but that's as far as this goes. Outrage over the lack of wedding bells is completely misplaced."

"First of all, it's *dinner*." Her voice had begun to shake with anger. "I didn't expect any skywritten proposals. But, wow, I thought you respected my work. I thought—" She had hurried to dress, stepping into the jeans she'd been wearing earlier and yanked on a pullover. Her hair had come loose from its clip and she'd flung the butterfly hinge across the room.

"Of *course*, I respect your work." Had he rolled his eyes a tiny bit? Yes. Because she was always so sensitive about it. She had talent by the truckload as far as he could tell, but she had zero confidence in herself. Fake it till you make it was his motto while she seemed to be nurturing a hard case of impostor syndrome.

She had sent him the most scorchingly bitter look he'd ever received from anyone. It had stung deep inside where he had believed he was well-guarded and impervious.

"For God's sake, Nina. I've bought you everything you need. What does that say about my belief in your potential?"

"So much," she choked out as she grabbed her phone from the top of the dresser and threw it into her day bag. She had flung the bag over her shoulder and hurried down the hall.

"We'll talk about it later, then?" he'd called facetiously.

She had spun around in the hall to face him. Her eyes had been glistening with angry tears. "No one has ever made me feel as stupid as you have tonight. Goodbye, Reve."

She hadn't come back. He'd check her social channels and seen she was with her father so he presumed she was staying at the hotel with him, and next thing he knew, she was in Albuquerque and had blocked him.

The penthouse had felt hollow and quiet after she was gone. He resented that she had conditioned him to expect someone to be waiting for him and, out of sheer aggravation, had had her things boxed up. He'd had his assistant track down her father's address, but at the last minute Reve had balked at shipping it to her.

She would come back for it. Designing clothes in New York was her dream. She'd put hours and hours of work into each piece.

Sell it. Give it away. Throw it away. I don't care, but it's not mine.

She didn't really mean that. She couldn't. If she did, it meant that she really hadn't intended to see him today.

His heart teetered at that thought, and he quickly steadied it. Her turning up here was one more act in a play. He wasn't being a misogynist thinking this was nothing but mind games and manipulations. Men did it too. Everyone did.

But he kept hearing her say, *You're actually the only person I can tell. Maybe the best person, because you have no emotional investment.*

No emotional investment. That was certainly the goal, but hearing it stated like a blunt fact, without any taunting inflection, made him sound like a sociopath.

He felt things. He just didn't allow those feelings to control him or allow him to be controlled by someone else.

She really believed he felt nothing, though. She had only come into his neighborhood to flip him off because she was still angry at how stupid he had made her feel.

It made him sick to think she'd felt belittled by him.

How had he not clued in to her trouble with reading? She almost always dictated her texts. When she did type one out, she used a lot of emojis. She had invariably asked him to order for her when they went for dinner, or listened to the specials rather than read the menu. She spent very little time on social media or browsing headlines, but she loved audio books and podcasts.

He'd thought she liked to listen because her hands were always busy. He hadn't realized she had had to work twice as hard as everyone else to master the basics. He'd grown up in poverty of all sorts, but he'd had a mind that grasped concepts quickly and he often took that for granted.

He had also taken for granted that Nina was as jaded and pragmatic as he was. He *wanted* her to be like him. That's how simple, harmless affairs remained simple and harmless.

He looked at her, so innocent and defenseless in her slumber. No one could get through life with their heart pinned on their sleeve the way she seemed to.

Don't fall for it, he warned himself.

Her phone burbled.

Nina snapped awake with a gasp and a disoriented look around.

When her gaze snagged on him, a glimmer of wonder touched her expression. A smile began to dawn.

A sensation he couldn't describe bloomed in his chest, but before it could take hold, memory seemed to steal all the light from her eyes. Her expression darkened the way a cloud blocked the sun. Whatever flame of possibility had sparked to life in her was doused and buried.

She swung her feet to the floor and picked up her phone. "It's my dad."

For one beat, there was only another burble from her phone while she stared expectantly at him.

"What?"

Nina abruptly rose and walked down the hall, swiping the phone to speaker as she went. "Hi, Dad."

"Hi, button, what's up?" Then, with sharp concern, "Where are you?"

"Reve's." Her voice was fading, but he heard the heavy sheepishness in his name.

"Nina." The older man's voice rang with fatalism. *"Why?"*

Reve didn't hear her reply. She shut herself into the spare bedroom while he sat there thinking, *Ouch.* Dad certainly didn't want to meet him *now*, did he?

That's when it struck him why Nina had looked at him so strangely a minute ago. He had always left the room when her family called. Always. She had expected him to walk away today. When he hadn't, she had.

He didn't know why that felt like such a knee to the groin, but it sure did.

Nina turned her face up to the spray of the shower, washing away tears as they leaked from her closed lashes.

"Nina?" Reve walked into the bathroom without knocking.

"Reve! I'm in the shower." *Obviously.* The walls of the cubicle were fogged and they used to shower together pretty much every day, but that wasn't who they were anymore. She crossed her arms over herself, feeling naked in more than just a physical way.

"Are you crying?" He closed the door and stood there as a blurry bulk, arms crossed.

"Yes." She regretted ever telling him she preferred to cry in the tub or shower. It was starting to freak her out how much he'd taken in and remembered about her when their last conversation had convinced her she was nothing to him. "Can you leave me to it?"

"Look, I'm sorry he's turning his back on you. I wish I had some good advice on how to handle that, but most people are garbage and this is why I don't let people close to me. I'm not *broken*. I just hate expecting better from people only to be disappointed when they let me down."

Dear Lord, that sounded like a tragic way to live. And this was how she'd tricked herself into thinking he needed her. A man with such a big cloud hanging over him needed sunshine peeking through.

"He's not turning his back on me. He was perfectly sweet. He already *knew*."

"And never told you?" He sounded outraged. "What an ass. No wonder you're upset."

"I'm *relieved*." Did he understand anything about how human beings worked? "I'll tell you what he said in a minute. Can you go? Please?"

He made a grumbling noise and left.

She finished up, combed out her wet hair and walked into the bedroom wearing only a towel.

Reve was in the chair, legs straight, ankles crossed. He was turning a small abstract sculpture in his hands.

She came up short, asking with exasperation, "What are you doing in here?"

"Do you have pink in your hair?" His hands stilled as he studied her. "It's cute."

"I'll tell my sister you like it. Could you wait in the living room?"

"This isn't new to me." He waved at her.

"That was basically my dad's reaction," she said ironically as she secured her towel. "Is my suitcase still by the door?"

"I brought those." He pointed at the foot of the bed.

She looked at the familiar ice-blue silk boxers and matching T-shirt. Her brightly colored kimono was there, too. She had made the set for herself and had worn them every morning when she had risen naked from his bed.

She touched the cool, sleek fabric. "Why do you still have these?"

"They were in the drawer. I never got around to sending them to storage with the rest." He shrugged off any significance.

"Has anyone else worn them?"

"*No.* Why would you ask that?" His mouth warped in insult.

"Well, I don't know, do I?" She gave a defensive shrug. "Thank you." She had slept in her pajamas on her friend's decrepit sofa the last few nights and would rather burn them than wear them again.

She took the shorts and top into the bathroom and left the door cracked as she changed behind it, talking as she did.

"I was almost a year old when Dad found out. He was running out of time to claim a life insurance benefit on—" She peered around the door. "I hate to say she wasn't my mother even though I never met her and she didn't give birth to me."

"'Kay." He was tossing the sculpture between his hands.

His gaze flickered to her bare legs as she came back into the bedroom, touching her ankles just long enough to pull warmth into all of her exposed skin, and then he met her gaze without remorse. In fact, there was a flickering flame of appreciation in his gaze.

She did her best to ignore it, but she was hideously conscious of the fact she was braless in silk and her nipples were hardening to press against the light-as-cobwebs fabric.

She shrugged on the kimono and tied it closed, her lower back tingling with the sense he was watching her every move.

"The insurance company called Dad to clarify because the copy of the death certificate he'd submitted didn't match the one they had requested from the government in Luxembourg. The government one had a box ticked that indicated his wife was pregnant at her time of death. They said that usually means she hadn't delivered. Dad had only seen her for a few seconds, just long enough to identify her because he had three kids right outside the door, one of them a newborn, the other two completely traumatized. The clinic took care of cremation, and the doctor called him with the autopsy results a few months later. Dad never saw the actual report, though. He told the insurance company he definitely had a baby, but by then I was starting to look not so much like them." She turned and waved at the door. "Can we—?"

She couldn't stay in such an intimate place while she told him all these intimate things.

He shrugged and rose, all of his masculine energy swirling around her, making her aware of their thin, loose clothing, and his height and strength and lazy regard.

She swallowed and picked up her phone before she led him to the living room, where her glass of wine sat on the coffee table.

She picked it up and wandered out to the terrace. The concrete still held the day's heat, and the setting sun turned the surrounding buildings to rose gold.

Reve joined her a moment later, having detoured for the bottle and his own glass.

"He was starting to have suspicions?" he prompted as he topped her up.

"Thanks," she murmured absently. "Yes. He didn't want to believe he'd brought home a stranger's baby, but had a paternity test done and discovered he had."

"Did he tell the clinic?" His focus on her was intense.

She'd always found Reve's full attention to be thrilling and disconcerting. It made her feel as though she was the only thing that mattered in the world.

Don't read into it, she warned herself, looking away. It had taken weeks to fully grasp that he'd only been using her for sex. He wasn't the charming, concerned protector that she had cast him to be.

"He left a few messages, but no one got back to him." She moved to the half wall that formed the rail of the terrace. Below her, shadows were collecting in Central Park. "Dad didn't want to rock too many boats, though. He told Abuela. He thought she deserved to know since she was raising her daughter's children while he was still flying for the air force. They were both afraid I'd be taken away if they revealed what had happened. Children get deported, too."

He grimaced an acknowledgment as he joined her.

"The little that Dad remembered about the clinic was that they handled discreet services for celebrities. He presumed I had been given up voluntarily by someone who couldn't keep me. He didn't want me to end up in some orphanage in Europe, forcing them to grieve another loss. He said Abuela said her daughter had made sure they had a baby to help them cope with losing her. She said I'd already brought her so much comfort and love that she couldn't bear to give me up."

Nina had to bite her lips to steady them. Abuela had been the only mother Nina had ever known. She had loved her with everything in her and missed her every single day.

Reve didn't say anything.

She glanced to find him watching her with intense concentration, but as she met his gaze, he turned his to the horizon and gave a light snort.

"You're such a product of the material world," she said with affront. "There are things that can never be seen or measured or proven, you know. If you believe they're real, they are. I thought it was a lovely thought that I was brought to them through her daughter's spirit."

"It is," he allowed. "And it's true I don't believe in ghosts or cosmic fate, but it was wrong of him to keep it from you. You shouldn't have found out like this."

"It's a really painful topic for him." Her father had cried openly as they had revisited the grim loss, breaking her heart. "He said the time never seemed right to bring it up, and he never wanted me to feel anything but his. He was pretty freaked-out that I might have a twin." She chuckled softly into her glass.

"What about the rest of your family?"

She sobered. "He's asking my brother to meet him at my sister's. He'll text as soon as he's spoken to them." She hoped they took the news as well as her father had. "You can make whatever statement you want after that." A searing sensation went from the base of her throat to the pit of her stomach. "And I'll get out of your hair."

CHAPTER FIVE

SHE REALLY HADN'T come here to pick up where they'd left off.

Reve wet his arid throat with wine, absorbing that.

"Where will you go?" he asked. "Back to Albuquerque?"

"Not if, um…" She swirled her wine and licked her lips. "Dad's going to call one of his air force buddies who became a commercial pilot. He keeps a flat in Frankfurt and has offered it to Dad in the past. Dad said he'd ask if I can use it. I feel so light now I've told him. Like I can *think*. Thank you for pushing me to call him."

She gave him the smile he'd been missing, the one that lit her up as though she had swallowed pure sunshine. She beamed it at him so hard his chest stung with the force of it.

"That's it, then? You'll leave in the next day or two?" He had the bizarre sensation of a bandage being peeled very slowly from his chest, taking one hair at a time and a layer of skin with it, but it was happening on the inside of his rib cage.

"Depending on flights, yes. I'm still eligible to fly military, but it's space available. I don't want to hang around here like bait for the photographers, so I might have to book commercial. And I have to look into whether I can work once I'm there," she said with a distracted frown. "I'm sure a bar or club would hire me for cash. At least I brought my passport. That interview was good for something," she said with another overbright smile.

He could already see ten things wrong with her plan, but her phone pinged with a text.

She moved across to peer down at where she'd left it faceup on a side table next to the settee. Whatever photo appeared on the screen made her shoot him an uneasy look.

"My brother." She tucked her hands into her neck as though her phone was a coiled snake she was being forced to pick up.

Chewing the corner of her mouth, she cautiously let one finger dart out to tap the screen. The AI voice read, "Marco. I love you, sis. Tell me what you need."

"Oh." Nina moved her hands to stack them over her heart. She glanced at Reve with eyes like exploding stars. Her mouth was a wobbly line. "Isn't he the best?"

Her phone pinged again. She tapped.

"Angela," the AI voice read. "I always knew you were special. Get a hotel on me. You don't have to stay with him. Call as soon as you're there. I want to hear everything."

"What have you been telling them about me?" Reve asked with offense.

Nina didn't meet his gaze as she picked up the phone and voice texted to both of them, "I love you both. I'll call as soon as I've figured out my next steps."

"You're not going to a hotel," Reve said when she lowered her phone. "The paparazzi will find you and we still have things to talk about."

"The press release? Say whatever you want, but it would be better if I wasn't here when you issue it, don't you think?" She polished her screen on her hip, then set her phone back on the table.

When she glanced at him, there was a deep vulnerability in her expression. Only a heartless bully would throw such a lamb to the wolves.

"We'll circle back to the press release. You know you don't have to go to Europe, right? I looked up Oriel while you were sleeping. Her new husband is a VP at TecSec. He'll want my business." The global security company had been on his radar for a while as an alternative to the one he was using. "I can make a call right now. He'll pick up."

"You don't want to be involved," she reminded, rolling her wine in the bowl of her glass. "I'm not sure *I* want to be involved. I mean, I do. I want to know if Oriel is my sister. I definitely want to meet her if she is, but…" She took a deep breath and slowly let it out. "I'm not ready to reveal myself. Oriel seems fine with the attention she's getting, but today's taste of it makes it seem pretty awful."

"It is. But you won't stay anonymous walking around with her face."

"There's nothing I can do about that, is there?" She paced down the length of the terrace and turned back, brows tugged into a wrinkle of consternation. "The problem is, I have questions that can't be answered by meeting her. She was legally adopted, but I was given to my father in a way that seems…opportunistic. As though someone was trying to hide me. That's weird, right? I'm not imagining it?"

He'd been thinking that, too. "It suggests criminal activity, yes." Which concerned him.

Her mouth tightened. "I keep thinking that right now is my only chance to poke around for answers, before whoever did this realizes I know who I am and starts to cover their tracks."

"Okay, but you can't go jabbing hornet nests without knowing what you're up against."

"I don't have *time* to take a more cautious approach." She pointed at her face. "This is a ticking clock."

"Hire someone," he threw out. "Tell your family to keep their mouths shut, lock down your social media and lie low. That buys you a little more time off the radar while you wait for a report."

"I don't know first thing about hiring a private investigator let alone have the money to pay for one. I certainly can't sit and watch game shows in a hotel room while they try to get answers to questions I've barely articulated."

"I'll pay for it." He shrugged that off.

"No, thank you," Nina bit out, cheekbones darkening with temper.

"Which brings us to something else we need to discuss." Ire prickled at him as he noted her hackles were rising. "Where did you get the idea you owe me for the things I bought you?"

"I already told you where I stand on this. You bought it. You own it." She walked past him and went inside, snapping the door back into place.

"For God's sake, Nina," he said as he followed her. "What are we even talking about? A few yards of silk and a few pairs of shoes?"

She flung around to face him, pronouncing spitefully, "Twenty-nine thousand, four hundred and seventy-eight dollars and sixty-eight cents. That might not be much to you, but it's a lot to me."

That took him aback. "You kept track of how much you spent?"

"Of course I did! I was always going to pay you back once I established myself."

"So why haven't you?" he asked with exasperation.

She jerked her head back.

"I mean, why haven't you continued trying to establish yourself? Put on a show. Get some orders. Find a factory to produce it. What the hell are you waiting for?"

"Oh, it's just that easy, is it?" Her face was crimson, her eyes wearing the glossy sheen of venomous fury she'd worn when she'd walked out on him. She looked to her phone, which was still outside, then her bag on the floor.

It made his stomach clench, but he kept pushing.

"All I did was underwrite your ambitions. Stand here and explain to me why that was such a crime."

"I may be thick, Reve, but even I know that sex work is a crime! Buying *and* selling. Thanks for implicating me in that because I wasn't aware that's why I was here." She chucked back the last of her wine and clanked her glass onto the bar top.

"How the hell do you make that leap? *How?*" he demanded, astounded.

"Oh, were you *in love* with me?" Her sarcasm held a rawness that scored deep into him. "Was that why you asked me to live with you? Because I *thought* you were. That's why *I* was here. I thought I was in love with you, Reve. Then I found out I was here to keep your bed warm. 'We're comfortable,'" she mocked. "'Why does it have to go anywhere?'"

Thought. He leaned back on his heels, sternum vibrating under the force of her anger and sense of betrayal.

He wouldn't have believed her if she had claimed to have actually been in love. Love was like the spirit that had guided her into her grandmother's tender arms—a nice thought, but mostly existing through acts of deliberate self-delusion.

He was starting to see that Nina was prone to that, though. She was a romantic, which made him the sort of person who took advantage of that, and he didn't like that view of himself one bit.

"I thought you wanted me to help you." He tried for a reasonable tone.

"And I thought you were helping me because you believed in me as an artist." She blinked fast. Even from across the room, he could tell her lashes were wet and matted. "You didn't care about my work, though. You wanted sex on tap."

"Not true. If all I wanted was a warm body in my bed, Kelly Bex would have been here. I want *you*, Nina." He pointed at her.

She took a step back.

Because he'd spoken in the present tense.

He ran his tongue over his teeth. He hadn't meant to reveal that, but yeah, his craving for her was circling him like a school of sharks. He kept batting his urges away because she was going through some stuff, but for one second he let her see it. He *wished* what he felt for her was the sort of base attraction any woman could satisfy. It wasn't. It had to be her.

Her expression twisted in confusion and she crossed her arms defensively.

"I wanted you to succeed," he insisted. "Maybe I don't know the fine points about fashion and trends, but I knew how hard you were working to have a voice in that world, how passionate you were about every stitch and pleat. Your sketches alone were enough to show me you had talent. Hell, Nina. I believe in you more than you believe in yourself."

"That is the most arrogant thing you have ever said in your life." Her arms shot straight down at her sides. "Which is saying a *lot*."

"Your dream was *right there*." He waved toward the hall. "And you walked away from it. You're still trying to walk away. That has nothing to do with me. If you want it, it's there. Quit making excuses and make it happen. But you're too afraid to pull the trigger. Aren't you?"

"What do you know about it? You think it's easy to put yourself out there?" Her arm flailed and she knocked her glass flying into the bar sink with a tinkle of broken glass. She made an infuriated noise, barely glancing at the damage. "It's not just ego, you know. Not for me." She smacked a hand onto her chest. "I've always had to do everything twice. Once my way, then I had to reverse engineer it so I could prove I knew how to do it the 'right' way." She made air quotes with her fingers. "Then Kelly picked apart everything I made."

So she could steal Nina's ideas. He'd watched her hurt and confusion as she saw her modified designs appear under Kelly's name.

"I've never understood why you let her get away with that."

"It was my first job in this industry! I thought I was *learning*." She touched her brow. "I thought I wasn't good enough yet and she was mentoring me, making me better."

Yet. That word encapsulated Nina's hopefulness and conviction in her ability to succeed, but where had her faith in herself gone?

"I was giving you a chance to do it your way, Nina."

"Because you wanted to have sex with me," she accused.

"Because I liked seeing you happy. What a jerk to want to put a smile on your face," he scoffed. "But even if I was doing it as a transaction, *so what*? Why would that matter if you were getting what you wanted?"

"Don't be gross!"

"I'm not being gross. I'm asking how badly you want that dream? Not bad enough to do whatever it takes to get it."

"Because I'm not like that," she cried.

"Like what? Ruthless? I am." He moved to pick up the cordless house phone. "If you don't want all those boxes of clothes you made, fine. I'll call Kelly, tell her to get them out of my storage locker."

"Oh, you just try it, you bastard. I'll—" She stormed right up on him, glowing with incendiary fury.

His heart nearly exploded in reaction to the threat rolling off her even as another part of him gloried in how magnificent she was.

"You'll what?" he invited, heart galloping. "Fight for it?"

"Yes, damn you, I will." She grabbed the phone out of his hand and blindly threw it.

It hit the coffee table, where it bounced and skittered to the floor, possibly breaking into pieces.

He didn't look. Their gazes were locked, and all of his senses were drinking her in. Her loose hair with its shocks of pink, fine strands lifting as if electrified. Her pupils were exploded so there was only a glow of dark gold around them. She breathed in uneven pants.

He could feel his teeth showing as he smiled in atavistic glee. He was hard, so freaking hard for her in an instant. His blood had become hundred-proof alcohol, sharp and hot in his arteries, searing through his system and making his head swim. All his logic and calculations of risk and brain cells melted into the simmering pool of testosterone he was drowning in.

"Are we doing this?" He barely recognized his voice it was so guttural and raw.

"Yes." She grabbed his head and dragged his mouth to hers, lifting her mouth to meet him.

His arms went around her, and he tried… He honestly tried not to ravage her. Her fists knotted in his hair, and the pain made him realize he was squeezing her with all his strength, but she wouldn't let him lift his head. Her teeth raked his lips and he knew they would both have bruises after. Maybe she would even break his skin, but he'd be damned if he would protest her kissing him as if she wanted to bite his lips from his face.

He ran his hands down to her ass and squeezed, bracing his feet in a signal that was so well practiced between them he didn't even think of what he was doing until her weight landed against him. Her breasts mashed into his chest as he absorbed the force with a single staggered step back.

Her arms looped behind his neck, and her legs wrapped tight around his waist. His muscles strained as he held her tight and kissed her again. Plundered. Swept his tongue into the hot, wine-flavored cavern of her mouth and sucked her tongue into his.

He wanted to take her to the sofa, the floor, against the wall. They were both making noises like animals landing prey after weeks of starvation.

He *was* starved. He'd been suffering deprivation since she had left, and he was furious with her for it. Did she think any woman would be good enough after he'd had her? No one had even tempted him.

Holding her tight, he strode into his bedroom.

Nina had forgotten—or blocked out—how good it felt to be held by him. How his strong arms made her feel as though he wanted to meld them into a single being.

The friction as he walked stimulated her in primitive ways. Their mouths met, tasted and tangled and pillaged. She knew she was making carnal noises. So was he. She could hardly breathe, but she didn't want to give up one second of having her mouth sealed to his. She started to feel herself being pulled away and scrabbled her hands against the hard cords of muscles across the tops of his shoulders, hanging on.

The mattress hit her back and his weight came down between her legs, knees pushing behind her thighs to shove her higher onto the mattress. He yanked her kimono open, his hands busy between them as he fought with her belt. She drove her hands into his hair, dragging him back to kissing the hell out of her.

He did, and then swept his mouth to her throat. She felt the sting of him planting a hickey against her skin and let a jagged, encouraging cry scrape from her throat. She arched and his touch slid under her top, up to her breast.

The sensation of his hot palm claiming the swell was so acute she lifted her hips and bit through the shoulder seam of his shirt just hard enough to express the intensity gripping her.

They were both being rough and greedy. She was, anyway, but she *needed* this. She needed to see his gaze come up blind with lust. When she moved her hands under his shirt, skating her fingertips over his hard abs and up to his tight nipples, she couldn't get enough of the light scour of hair against her palms. She drank in the sight of him closing his eyes and smiled as she felt him shake under her touch.

He rocked onto his elbow and pushed her top up, baring her stomach as he slid down to open his mouth across her belly, taking soft, wet bites. He kissed his way up to the underside of her breast, pushing her top up to expose her, causing heat to swirl through her and lewd craving to pulse between her legs.

Their clothes kept getting in the way, but she didn't want to stop to undress and he didn't seem to want that, either. He captured her nipple and gave a strong, wet pull, drawing another keening cry from her. She wrapped her arms around his head and held him there, tortured by the delirious pleasure he was bestowing on her.

As he moved to her other breast, his hand went under her back, slid into her silk shorts at her tailbone and started to push them off. As they went down her thighs, so did he, his mouth kissing wetly down and down as though called there.

"Reve," she gasped, trying to pull her ankle free of the silk.

He used two fingers to part her folds, the way he'd always done, and set his mouth to her bared flesh. He paused—one breath, two—waiting for her to catch up to the intense heat and acute sensations. Waiting for her to want the circle of his tongue. Waiting for her to get over her moment of shyness and relax into this caress.

As she shivered and instinctually lifted her hips, spearing her hand into his hair, inviting him, he settled in to pleasure her with his clever tongue.

It was everything she remembered and more. Sharp streaks of pleasure went down the insides of her thighs. Tension coiled in her belly. It was so good, so good, but not enough.

"I want—" She tried to roll to the nightstand.

He rose and reached.

"And the stuff."

He handed her the lube and stood on his knees over her, pushing his shorts down only far enough to bare his erection so he could roll on a condom.

She spread cool gel across latex and he stole a dollop, touching her shoulder in a signal to lie back. He worked the slippery coolness into her and it nearly made her cry. She had missed his touch so much. She had missed the way they knew each other's bodies and spoke without words. He knew exactly how to press and tease and make her gasp with pleasure.

It had been so painful to lose that a latent sob throbbed from her throat.

"Hurt?" He started to withdraw his touch.

"No. I want you in me so *much*." She beckoned him to cover her again. She guided him herself, closing her eyes as she lined him up.

She wasn't completely ready. There was a pinch as he pressed for entrance. It made her shiver but, oh, it felt good to have him filling her, so thick and hot and hard.

He was swearing, eyes glazed. She could feel him shaking with an effort to hold himself in control.

"Don't be gentle." She let her nails bite into his buttocks, then drew her knees up to his rib cage. "I'm really so close."

With a groan, he kissed her open mouth with his own, lascivious and proprietary. Then he began to move with firm thrusts, watching her through slitted eyes.

She was so aroused, so ravenous for his powerful body moving in hers, she met his thrusts with lifts of her hips, encouraging him to let go. It was raw and gratifying and made her breaths shorten.

Her grip on him tightened. He increased his tempo. The sensations redoubled, and she slipped into a place of pure pleasure that seemed to have no peak, only more and more hot joy as all of her awareness narrowed to that point of potential inside her. She tensed, reaching. "Don't stop. Harder. *Please…*"

She shattered. All of her exploded into a thousand

pieces while he roared and pinned his bucking hips to hers. His iron-hard arms caged her tight while he groaned into her neck and pulsed deep within her.

CHAPTER SIX

AFTER AN EON, when she floated in a space devoid of thought, Nina realized she needed a full breath. She touched his shoulder.

Reve dragged in his own breath, as though preparing himself for supreme effort, then carefully withdrew. In the same motion, he rolled to grab the box of tissues, offering it to her, exactly as he had always done.

Still dazed, Nina took two and used them while he removed the condom. He took the tissues from her and dropped them into the bedside wastebasket with the condom. He lay back beside her with a heavy sigh. He pulled his shorts into place before tugging his shirt down over them.

Her shorts were still on the floor somewhere. She closed the kimono and stayed beside him, stunned by what had just happened. It had been good, *so* good. Fast and…necessary? Probably not. Inevitable, she supposed.

Her own exhale was weighted with despair.

His head turned on the mattress. They were both still crooked on the bed.

"Made it longer than I expected." She looked to the clock as an excuse to turn her face away. "Almost six hours."

"And may have set a land speed record." His humor was as thin as hers, the edges brittle.

She pressed the back of her head into the mattress and looked at the familiar ceiling, trying not to cry. Why hadn't it been awful? Why didn't she feel dirty so she could hate him and hate herself and leave without ever looking back?

Instead, she felt as she always had, as though he knew her in ways she didn't even know herself. As though, together, they were greater than the sum of their parts.

It was just sex, though. Really, really good sex, but sex all the same.

"Do you want to stay here?" he asked. "Instead of a hotel?"

"Here?" She pointed at the mattress. She should have seen that coming. "No," she pronounced disdainfully.

"In the apartment," he clarified with equal condescension.

"Why would you even offer? Don't turn this into more than it was." Good advice for herself. She sat up and scooted to the edge of the bed.

"What was it?"

The spiteful thing to say would be, *Why does it have to be anything?*

"I don't know." She folded her arms across her middle, where an empty ache reached from the bottom of her stomach to the top of her heart. "I'd love to say stress relief, but I think I needed to feel like that again, to remind myself there was a reason I fell for you. We were really good for a little while and there's no shame in enjoying that. Is there?"

She peeked over her shoulder at him.

His gaze was flinty, his face shuttered and hard.

"So this was closure?" His lip curled.

Her lungs were filled with powdered glass. She looked forward again, unutterably sad. "Yes."

"Fine."

The word knocked the stuffing out of her, leaving her so bereft her whole body went numb.

He sat up beside her. "But that means dealing with your things."

"I told you—" She dug her heels into the rail of the bed, propped her elbows on her thighs and held her palms over her eyes.

"I believe you were threatening my life if I disposed of it without your input?" he reminded in a falsely friendly tone.

"Don't give it to her. Anyone but her," she begged, still hiding behind her hands.

"Who then?"

"I don't know," she moaned. "No one wants a cardboard box full of some unknown designer's blood, sweat and tears. I'll ship it home to Dad, I guess."

"Quit being such a coward."

She dropped her hands and glared at him.

His brows went up to a pithy angle. "Yes, that's what I called you."

"Oh, okay. I'll just throw together a show, then. Getting media attention won't be any problem! But I'll forever wonder if any success I have is mine or because of the stranger I happen to resemble, won't I?"

He stared down at her for so long she started to shrink under the weight of his penetrating gaze.

"That really bothers you, doesn't it?" he said with a baffled snort. "Most people would use every advantage to get what they want." He shook his head as though it didn't make sense to him.

"I told you, I'm not like that."

"I'm starting to believe that. I also think you're using it as an excuse not to try."

"Reve!" She stood up, angry and hurt, sweeping her hand out in helpless confusion. "Look at my life right now. I don't have time to reboot my failed career. Even if I tried to put together a show, it wouldn't be how I had planned it. The themes would be all wrong. My entire sense of self has changed. I don't know who I am anymore."

Even as frustrated tears burned behind her eyes, another part of her latched on to her own words. Maybe that could be the message. Any collection would be a snapshot of her life, not all of it. Sometimes things happened, forcing a detour. If a goal was important enough, you came back and picked up the pieces and tried a new approach...

Concepts began to swirl in her imagination. She was warming to it, playing with it.

"I know that look. You're thinking about it," he said smugly.

"So?" She tightened the belt of her kimono and began to pace. "I still don't have time. I don't have money." She threw up a hand at him. "Don't."

"I *will* offer to underwrite it and I'll tell you why." He rose, hair mussed, clothing wrinkled, and sexy as hell with his powerful muscles and stern jaw. "I refuse to let you boot this down the road or cobble it together on a shoestring and say you tried. I'll hire someone to do it right, pay for the show and take eighty percent of net profit in lieu of you paying me back for any of it."

"That's ridiculous."

"Seventy-five."

"I'm not arguing the percentage! Take eighty percent of zero. See if I care."

He swore under his breath. "I might get twelve dollars. I might get twelve million. That's called investing."

She shook her head and walked toward the window. "Don't."

"Don't what? Believe in you more than you believe in yourself?"

She stopped and spun and huffed an annoyed noise at the way he kept throwing that in her face.

"You only need one order for one piece, Nina. If it's big enough, I could make tenfold what I've invested in you so far."

"You always talk like these things are easy. Get a grip on the real world, Reve! Even if I did get an order, I would have to source the fabrics and find a factory. Get it made, get it here. At a profit. It's not *one thing*."

"So I wouldn't get my money tomorrow. That's also called investing. I know how to get a business off the ground, Nina—in the real world," he snarled. "I've had to do it many times. You need capital to set up shop and put a supply chain in place. That's what I'm offering you."

"I need to figure out who I *am*."

"You're not a fashion designer? An artist? That always seemed to be at the core of your identity."

It was, but… "Why are you pushing me like this? Do you want my stuff out of your storage locker that badly?"

"I want it out from between us," he said forcefully, pointing at the stretch of floor that separated them.

He seemed as startled by those vehement words as she was. He stood straighter and glanced away, jaw clenched.

"Why?" she asked helplessly. "Because of that?" She pointed at the bed.

"No." He pulled a wrinkle from the bedspread and then dropped the lube back in the drawer. He kept his back to her. "No one gave me a leg up or looked out for me in any way. That's all I want to do, Nina. Maybe I wasn't the best *boyfriend*." He drawled the word as if it was too puerile a label for what he'd been to her. It was. "Maybe I looked on your being here as a convenient arrangement, not…" His fingers tapped on the night table as he seemed to search for words.

"Not a relationship with a future, but I do care what happens to you."

He turned. His expression was difficult to interpret. He was too self-confident to be defensive. Guarded, maybe?

She swallowed, but the scoured feeling behind her breastbone remained. She had spent months backpedaling through their relationship, taking all of his small kindnesses and thoughtful gestures and reframing them as quid pro quos for sex. Despite the very good sex they'd just had, he didn't owe her anything, not even a night's sleep in a comfortable bed. There was no reason for him to keep after her this way beyond the reason he was giving—that he wanted to support her aspirations.

Maybe he always had.

Her eyes grew hot with unshed tears. She bit her lips to keep them from trembling.

"I don't think you should fly off to Germany by yourself to hunt down potential criminals," he said, squeezing the back of his neck. "At least let me hire someone to go in for a discreet recon. Stay here while you figure out flights and make a plan. My security is watertight. You can organize a show while you're here."

"And you would give me all this support why?" she asked with a husky laugh of disbelief. "So we can part as friends?"

"We'd be business partners," he corrected.

"You *want* that?"

"Why not?"

"Because it's impossible! I'll wind up in bed with you." She waved at the bed as proof. "And you don't want the sort of future that I want."

"Which is what? Marriage? Children?"

"Yes," she said firmly, though it felt like a very far-off, abstract goal right now. It had always been in her realm of expectation that her life would include making a family with a man she loved, but as she sank down into the overstuffed chair in the corner, she wondered what the new Nina would want once she came out the other side.

It struck her that these were her final moments as Nina Menendez, the woman she'd always known herself to be. Soon she would be Oriel Cuvier's sister or Lakshmi Dalal's daughter. Everything would be different.

Reve was offering her the gift of being herself a little longer.

Damn him, he shouldn't be making this into such a difficult decision. She had sworn to her family that she wasn't coming back to New York to see him. He was bad for her. So bad that she had just slept with him. Obviously, she couldn't be trusted around him.

On the other hand, she didn't want to rush into the unknown, turning over rocks at random. She needed a plan. She wasn't actually that good in new places, sometimes confusing her directions. And the signposts would be in different languages, which would be even harder for her to read than English. Her father couldn't afford private investigators, but she saw the sense in hiring one.

"I would want to know how much you spend," she said cautiously. "One way or another, I want to pay you back for—"

"I'll make some calls." He walked out before she could say anything more.

Reve was a man of action. Moving, shaking, tearing down and rebuilding gave him the illusion he had control over his life. Back when he'd had little to no say over what happened to him, he'd achieved small triumphs in bashing rusted nuts from a wheel so he could get at the brake parts or by puzzling out how the water pump was installed so he could remove it.

As long as he'd worked toward a goal of some kind, he hadn't been standing still in the run-down shack that had held an alcoholic father and an empty refrigerator. At the very least, staying busy had allowed him to forget his empty stomach for a while.

He issued his statement that he'd never met Oriel Cuvier and began making calls for Nina's show. As he did, he realized this was an ironic version of his long-held coping strategy—he was trying to forget her desire for "closure" by providing it for her.

It made for an itchy, irritable sensation within him, but he got the ball rolling. Otherwise, he would sink into reliving their flurry of lovemaking.

Then the memory arrived anyway, running over him like a mile-long train and, *damn*, that had felt good. He was embarrassed by how little finesse he'd shown, but she'd matched every greedy caress and every scorching kiss. It had been exciting as hell and over far too quickly. He wanted to say, *Let's try that again. Take it slow. Do it right.*

Do what right?

Don't turn this into more than it was.

Her dismissal of their lovemaking had been jarringly close to what he had said. *Why does it have to go anywhere?* That had sent her running back to Albuquerque.

Guilt crept into his consciousness like fleas under his shirt, itching and biting and driving him to prove something to her. Prove what? That he really did want her to succeed with her dream? He did, but it went deeper than that.

He hadn't realized how many inner hurdles, along with the external ones, she'd had to overcome. He knew something about not feeling good enough. It ate at him to know she was still struggling with that. That he'd contributed to it by believing she was as driven by self-interest as everyone else in his sphere.

He was still skeptical that anyone could be *that* honest and empathetic and warm, but he couldn't deny that she was in a very vulnerable position. Thinking of the hyenas of the press getting hold of her caused an overwhelming protectiveness to rise up in him.

It killed him to see the defeat in her eyes. The uncertainty. He was compelled to do something to build her up, to help her get back the joy she'd felt in her work. He felt good taking these steps on her behalf, as though it forged something between them. Not an obligation, but a connection. One that wouldn't break the minute she walked out again.

He clenched a fist, disturbed by how much the thought of her leaving filled him with dread. *Loneliness*.

He brushed the childish emotion aside. Solitude meant autonomy, that's why he preferred it. He wasn't trying to cling. He was trying to be a decent person. If helping her kept her under his roof a few days, fine. At least he got some home cooking out of it.

By the middle of the next morning, Reve was showing her a two-thousand-square-foot loft in Chelsea that made Nina have to pick her jaw up off the hardwood floor. The row of windows that ran the length of the narrow space provided amazing light. It was perfect!

A man named Andre, who organized fashion shows for some of the top designers, signed an NDA before he met them there. He smiled warmly when he saw Nina.

"Oriel! I wondered who the mystery designer was. It's so good to see you again." He walked forward, trying to embrace her.

"I'm, um, Nina Menendez." She pushed her hand between them, offering to shake.

He fell back on his heel and dipped his chin as though she was pulling his leg.

"Really," Nina assured him. "I'm not her. I believe she's currently with her husband in India."

"You look *exactly* like her." His confused gaze

went to the pink streaks in her hair and her deliberately bare face and dressed-down jeans and T-shirt.

"I've heard that before." Nina shrugged as if it was a mild nuisance that meant nothing. "It's one of the reasons I'm keeping such a low profile. I don't want to be seen as trading on our resemblance. I want my work to stand on its own."

"Of course."

Reve left to finalize the lease agreement. After thirty minutes of discussion with Andre, Nina was confident they were on the same page creatively. By that afternoon, Andre's well-versed team had arrived and Nina was unpacking her work from the boxes. There would be no models and catwalk, but along with a set designer and lighting technician, Andre planned to bring in a photographer, a digital marketing expert and a communications specialist to ensure maximum exposure.

The costs were adding up so fast they made Nina hyperventilate. The rent alone was twenty-five hundred a day, which Reve shrugged off.

"I paid more for that garden party I didn't attend."

She searched his expression, still having trouble believing he was willing to gamble this sort of money on her, but from things he'd said about past deals, some in the hundreds of millions, this was small potatoes.

Even so, she couldn't stand the idea of failing and causing him to take a loss. She worked sixteen-hour days, lingering long after Andre and his crew had left, adding finishing touches so her show would be ready by the end of the week. She probably would have slept there if Reve hadn't been in his car when it arrived every night at ten, texting her that dinner was waiting and he was hungry.

She also probably would have slept with him if he'd invited her to his bed, but he didn't. She ought to be glad for that, she supposed, but she was a little hurt that he was suddenly treating her like a professional acquaintance.

That's not how she was thinking of him. Despite her exhaustion, she lay awake every night, longing to go down the hall and lose herself in their special brand of passion.

When she did fall asleep, she woke abruptly to anxious thoughts—worries about whether the investigator was learning anything and whether she'd be okay at the loaned flat in Germany.

She worried about how she would say goodbye to Reve again. It had been a lot easier when she had been angry and hurt.

"Why are you up so early?" He came into the kitchen wearing only pajama bottoms and a night's worth of stubble. His voice held morning rasp that was intimate enough to awaken her erogenous zones, even as his morning erection was subsiding against the loose fabric of his pants.

She moved to the coffeemaker to hide the fact she'd noticed, but her cheeks were stinging and her voice was strained. "Early bird avoids the paparazzi. I asked your driver last night if he minded. He said it was fine."

"Anything before seven a.m. is double time. Of course, he doesn't mind," he said drily.

"Oh. Shoot." She faltered in rinsing out her travel mug. "I'll add it to my expenses."

"Don't worry about it." He moved to the cupboard and took out bread for the toaster.

They were back-to-back, and she was so aware of him that all the cells in her body seemed to align like magnets finding north. She could have stood there forever, basking in this closeness.

She swallowed and picked up the tea towel to dry her mug. "I didn't mean to wake you."

"I wanted to talk to you. I need to go to Europe."

"Today?" A zing of loss jolted through her, rooting her feet to the floor. She wasn't ready to say goodbye.

"Soon. There's a company I want to acquire." Dishes rattled as he set out a plate and a butter knife. "We already have some capability for making car parts with 3D printers, but this German outfit is taking it to the next level."

"Oh." With a shaky hand, she poured the espresso she'd made for herself into a mug for him. When she caught his eye, she found him watching her.

Her pulse leaped in reaction, and her gaze took an involuntary inventory of his wide shoulders and relaxed biceps, the muscled pecs with small dark nipples and his sectioned abs.

"I can be out of your hair anytime. Dad heard back from his friend. He's leaving his key with his neighbor. Dad wasn't able to get me on a flight, but I've looked at what's available. I just have to pick one and book it."

"I'm not kicking you out." Reve sent her a disgruntled scowl and yanked open the refrigerator. "I'm saying I could take you with me. When were you thinking of leaving?"

Her inner Reve-addict jumped on that suggestion, particularly as lust was trying to take hold in her, but she made herself say, "That's not necessary. You're doing too much already."

"It's nothing. I'm going anyway. I usually stay at my apartment in Paris. You can stay with me, same as we have been here."

Platonically?

Her sister had been alarmed when she learned Nina was staying with Reve. And that they'd had sex.

Nina, it's fine if you forgive him. It's fine if you believe he never meant to mislead you. But your eyes are open now. Don't let him hurt you again. Where are you two going if you start up again? You have a right to ask those questions.

Angela was right, but Reve didn't seem to be taking anything for granted. She almost wished he would pressure her into an affair so she could succumb, then blame him for her own weakness.

"I might get recognized in Paris," she pointed out.

"You might get recognized anywhere. That's why my apartment is a good option. It's more secure than some pilot's walk-up in Frankfurt."

"How long is the train from Paris to Luxembourg?"

"Three or four hours." The toast popped and he turned to butter it.

She screwed fresh grounds into place in the espresso machine. "Could we leave Friday?"

"*This* Friday? The day your show opens? Don't you want to be there?"

"Gawd, no."

"Why not?" He frowned at her.

"Fear." She curled her lip in disgust at herself.

"Chicken," he chided, then offered her the plate with the buttered toast. "Eat. I suspect you've been skipping lunch. Would you trust Andre to break everything down?"

"Yes. Maybe. I don't know what to think of him anymore." She took one slice. "He said something that freaked me out."

"What?" Reve clacked the plate onto the island and the second piece of toast nearly slid off it. His demeanor had gone from morning lazy to protective Neanderthal so quickly she could hardly swallow the bite of toast in her mouth.

"It wasn't anything mean." She cleared her throat, then turned to finish making her coffee one-handed. "It was actually encouraging, but I'm terrified he's deluding both of us. He said he would cover the cost of leaving the show up an extra week if I gave him the green cocktail dress. I told him about my deal with you and that I would ask."

She sent Reve a sideways look as she set the machine to gurgling and hissing.

His brow furrowed. "Can you alter that dress to fit him? He's a pretty big guy."

"He wants it as an investment." This was the part that sounded like a delusion. "He thinks in a year, once my work has had a chance to circulate and build momentum, an original piece by Nina Menendez will go for, um…" She could hardly say it. "Five figures."

"Is that a fact." Reve leaned his hips on the counter and folded his arms. "If I had known that, I might have kept it in my storage locker."

"Ha ha." She rolled her eyes.

"I'm not joking." He cocked his head. "Does he know about your connection to Oriel?"

"*No*. He probably suspects, but he genuinely likes the dress. He's been super honest with me about all of my work. If he thinks I played it too safe or missed an opportunity to elevate a piece, he says so, but he doesn't want me to change anything. He says it shows my evolution. He uses words like 'inspiring' and 'exciting.' I can't *bear* to see his face when he discovers no one else likes any of it." She was having flashbacks to Kelly's tight smiles and bitchy nitpicking after a fellow seamstress had gushed over something Nina had made. "Being across the Atlantic when the doors open sounds ideal."

"You big, giant chicken," he accused, but his tone was gentle and the curl of his mouth held affection.

That smile put the sweetest joy in her heart, an expansive feeling that made her feel shy and emotive and happy.

His gaze touched her mouth and sexual tension crackled.

He swallowed and picked up his coffee. "If you change your mind and want to stay, let me know. Tell him I'll call to work out something for the dress."

She nodded, releasing a low breath, disappointed.

Reve had been working long hours to keep his mind— and hands—off Nina. Every evening, after he'd gone home and worked out to the point of physical failure, he'd gone to collect her, texting from the street so she could slip in beside him undetected.

She always sagged with weariness, which helped him keep from making a pass, but he didn't like seeing her push herself so hard. He knew how much this meant to her, though, and that she was trying to keep her mind off what would happen once she went to Europe.

Reve had hoped his investigator would turn up more, saving her from going to Luxembourg herself, but the village had been overrun with reporters when Oriel's story broke. Apparently, the locals were being very tight-lipped. The man had at least located a property that was still in the family of the doctor who had delivered Nina.

Reve had taken a small liberty with that information, still concerned with what would happen to Nina once her story broke. He couldn't leave her to fend for herself, not when he had the resources and experience to buffer her from the worst of the attention.

At the same time, he knew he was setting up

himself—and her—for a rehash of his unsavory past if he let himself become part of her story. It disturbed him how much he was leaving himself exposed and why. He'd been blinded by sexual infatuation the first time with her and, yes, he still was. Despite working his body to quivering fatigue every day, he woke in the night so hard for her his whole body ached. Knowing she was just down the hall was pure torture, but there was a primitive, possessive part of him that liked having her close even if he couldn't touch her. Plus, he knew no other man was touching her.

Ah, jealousy. The most manipulative emotion of all. He fairly groaned aloud as he realized how susceptible he'd become to it.

Did she realize how much power that gave her over him? She would, he thought with a dour look at the champagne he'd picked up on his way to collect her. He was practically advertising it.

But he was here now, literally turning into the block where the showroom was located. It was Thursday, and Nina had texted that the photographer was coming at seven and she would be ready to leave after that. Reve had purposely arrived at six thirty.

He went inside for the first time since the day he'd leased the space, and could hear Nina and Andre bantering good-naturedly as he neared the cloakroom at the top of the stairs.

"See Now, Buy Now is everything that is wrong with today's world, not just fashion," Andre bemoaned. "It's the *manufacture* of trends. There's nothing organic or artistic about it. Why even bother— Oh, hello." Andre stopped dialing the switch that controlled the dimming of a track light. He poked his head into the showroom. "Nina, the most dashing man has turned up with champagne and only two glasses. I think that means one of us is supposed to take a walk."

"What? Reve!" Nina appeared with a flushed smile that struck the backs of his eyes like sunshine, but she used her body to forestall his entering the showroom, which prickled his old, suspicious instincts.

From here, all he could see was a table set up in front of a window. On it was an ornate business card holder that looked like an antique from a French chateau, a cup of pens and a single rose in a silver vase.

"Text me when the photographer gets here. I'll come back and close up after him," Andre said as he put on a tailored green jacket.

Nina thanked him for all his help and they embraced, kissing each other's cheeks.

As Andre stepped back, he said to Reve in a falsely pleasant tone, "If you spill one drop of that in my showroom, I will hunt you down and kill you with my bare hands."

Reve thumbed the cork so it popped loudly and fell to the floor. Only a wisp of condensation emerged from the neck.

"So long as we understand each other." Andre smirked and trotted down the stairs.

"This is a nice surprise. Thank you." Nina smiled nervously as he handed her a glass crackling with a head of bubbles.

"I thought I'd come see—" He stopped short of saying *what I've paid for.* "How it all came together."

They touched glasses and sipped, but she didn't move from the doorway. Her eyes grew wide and anxious. Panic-stricken.

"What's wrong? I've seen all of it before."

"Not like this."

"Like what?" She drove him a little crazy sometimes, being this emotionally attached to what? His opinion? "I'll be kind, Nina."

"I don't want you to be kind," she said, instantly cross. "I want you to be honest. I just don't know if I can handle it." She drained her champagne in a couple of swallows and set the glass on the shelf next to the bottle. "He's serious about no food or drink in there."

Reve seared his own throat with the cool, sizzling Salon Le Mesnil Brut and set his glass beside hers.

She jerkily waved him in ahead of her, then trailed behind him as he entered the long room. Tall tables and a couple of benches had been set up on the side of the room with the windows, probably to provide a space for buyers to sit and make notes or calls. The blinds on the windows were down, the showroom lit with lights that angled and pooled to guide focus.

The clothes were arranged down the inside wall and told a story that felt familiar to him since Reve recognized so many of the pieces. Still, it was a story he hadn't fully understood until now.

The first few outfits were pinned to cloth-covered squares that hung on the walls. Sketches were pinned alongside them, showing how the pieces had first been conceived. Each was pretty and well constructed. The lines were straight, the buttons were scrupulously spaced. They were undoubtedly good quality and classic—and very safe. There was an innocence to them. A hesitation.

As he ambled along, however, the sketches and outfits grew more daring. Brighter colors mingled with contrasting textures. Here, the clothing was draped over chairs and displayed on hangers that created an impression the pieces had begun to breathe and find life.

He remembered Nina being the same as she gained confidence in what she was trying to say and do. Her growing excitement had been evident in the way she had begun to stray from strict symmetry and played with adding a bracelet or sewing on a spangled pin.

Now he stood among mannequins in polished ensembles fit for high-powered boardrooms and elite social events. There was a white pantsuit with a wide-brimmed hat, the green cocktail dress with its gold chain belt and spiked heels. A yellow top with a sharply pointed collar was accented by a long-strapped purse and sexy sunglasses. A frozen wrist was cocked to hold a jacket and a marble leg kicked out the slit of a cheeky ruby skirt.

Standing among these pieces felt as though he was at a party, one where everyone was having the time of their life.

The fun then ended abruptly.

A gown of silver and blue sat upon a dress form with sequins only partially applied to its neckline.

The waist gaped because it was attached by dozens of pins, not stitches. One sleeve of the gown hung lifeless from the sewing machine beside it.

On the floor, among spilled sequins and scattered pins, a pair of designer shoes looked as though they'd been kicked off as the owner fled like Cinderella from her ball.

It was jarring, but even more so was the empty space that followed. A beam of light emphasized the emptiness. It shouldn't have felt like such a blow to the heart, but it was. He was responsible for that absence of work. Guilt settled as a bitter taste in the back of his throat. Loss. He had hurt her with his callousness that day. Hurt her so badly she had stopped doing what she loved and run away from her dream.

He had to close his eyes to absorb the pain that enveloped him.

He kept wanting to paint her actions with ulterior motives, but that was his own defense mechanism. The truth was this was who she was—a sensitive, emotive artist who only wanted to add beauty to the world. She was so raw and honest she had put her entire soul on display for the world to see.

She had shown it to him, and he hadn't appreciated what a privilege that was. It scared him that she was this open, it really did. Did she not realize how badly she could be hurt?

Bad enough she could walk away and tell him to *burn* all of this.

His nostrils stung as he drew in a breath. He wanted to take her into his arms, pour himself around her so nothing could touch her, but when he opened his eyes, he was looking at the dress she'd worn the day she'd come running back into his life.

It was a simple blue thing hung on a clear torso suspended from the ceiling—no head or accessories. It seemed to drift in midair like an apparition and was symbolic of her lost self, he supposed, with a hollow ring in his heart. The sense of something unfinished or unfound left a coil of deep longing inside him. It made him want to help her discover the rest of herself because he couldn't bear how insubstantial and adrift this suggested she was. As though she was only a shell of the woman she used to be, untethered.

The blue fabric was light enough to show the small bloodstain she must have brushed onto it that day. Despite that, and despite the fact it wasn't fancy or glamorous, he saw the small details that made it unmistakably part of the collection. Part of *her*, still alive and showing through. The skirt had a sophisticated flare that eschewed restrictions. There were crisscrossed straps at the back that had been hidden by her hair. They suggested a quiet defiance of convention, almost like graffiti that claimed, *I was here*.

Beyond that dress was a table piled with bolts of silk and linen and velvet in an array of colors. Ribbons and lace fell in coils from the top of it like ribbons off an unopened present. A pair of scissors sat atop a sketchbook open to a blank page.

Reve backed onto a bench and sat down, blowing out a low breath as though he'd been through something intense. His elbows went onto his knees and he rubbed his jaw before letting his gaze flicker back over the display.

"Is it too on the nose?" Nina asked with dread.

"Shh," he murmured, and absently took her hand.

He drew her to sit beside him, and his thumb played across her knuckles as his gaze slowly retraced the journey from the door to the unused fabrics. Finally he swiveled his attention to her, and the fierce light in his gaze made her heart pound in her chest.

"I don't know how to take this." She drew her hand from his and tangled her fingers over the unsteady sensation in her middle. "Are you appalled that you've thrown your money away? It's okay. Just say it."

"Nina," he breathed. "This is what you want." He pointed at the bench. "To knock people onto their ass." He spoke in a tone that was stunned—moved, even.

Her insides squirmed harder and her eyes grew damp.

"You're just being nice," she dismissed, pushing her hands between her knees and anxiously looking over what she feared was a vanity project.

"Stop it." He rose and pointed back to the beginning, his tone sharpening. *"Look* at what you've done. You *made* this." His arm swept the whole collection. "And you know what? I'm *proud* that I had something to do with it. *That* pisses me off," he said, pointing to the empty space. "Don't let anyone have that kind of power over you. *Especially me.*"

Too late, she thought, her heart squeezing as she

watched how he ran his hand over his jaw, his gaze agonized as he stared into the dust motes dancing beneath the empty spotlight.

"I hate that I had anything to do with you losing even one minute of pursuing your dream, but the rest? If you want to run yourself down, you're going to have to find someone else to listen to it because no, Nina. This is better than I expected and I expected a *lot*."

"Well, don't make me *cry*," she wailed. Although she had wanted his approval, his admiration, hearing it was too much to handle. It made her vision blur as tears soaked her lashes.

"You're crying because you're tired, you silly woman."

She was tired, but this was about him and how much it meant to her. When he caught her by the wrists and tugged her into his arms, she went there gratefully, still trembling in reaction.

"I didn't realize, Nina." His breath tickled against her hair, and his voice wasn't quite steady. "I didn't realize you have no filter or shield, that what you show the world and what you showed me, is actually *you*. That's too much. You know that, don't you?"

His hand clenched in her hair behind her neck. He drew back to search her eyes.

"It's who I was," she acknowledged, glancing at the floating dress. "And I had to say goodbye to her."

She'd been coming to terms with that all week. She would always have a home with her family, but the life she'd had with them in Albuquerque would never be the same. New York was no longer a place of promise where her dreams were yet to be realized. Even the artist who had imagined these pieces and turned them into reality was gone. She had felt it as she reacquainted herself with them. She still yearned to design and create, but she already knew her future work would be different. Her priorities had shifted. *She* had.

Even her visions of what she might have had with Reve were gone. Oh, she hoped they could continue this—affectionate embraces and a thread of trust—but she knew now that this was all they ever would have. At best, they were business partners with a past—hopefully friends—but they weren't lovers… and they would never be soul mates.

"Thank you," she said. "For not throwing this away. For giving me the means to make it in the first place, and for nudging me into taking this chance. No matter what happens with it, I'm grateful."

He cupped the side of her face, his thumb moving restlessly against her cheek as he searched her eyes. He started to dip his head and then stopped himself. His mouth pulled down at one side in self-deprecation.

She wanted that kiss. Yearned for it. She went onto her tiptoes and he met her halfway.

They clashed like storm waves to a shore, forceful and beautiful and thrilling. It was the most painful kiss of her life and the most tender. Her dream was all around her, in large part thanks to him. She poured her heart into their kiss, trying to convey what it meant to her to tell her story. What *he* meant to her.

His breath hissed and his hands moved over her with strength, but in a way that cherished, making her feel precious and needed and safe even as her soul was bared for all to see.

Just as passion started to flare, as they canted their heads to deepen the seal of their lips, a distant bell sounded.

Reve jerked his head up and his arms tightened protectively around her.

"It's the photographer," she said, pulling away to press the back of her hand to her buzzing lips. "For the…things." Her brain couldn't find words.

Footsteps paused in the cloakroom, probably as the champagne was spotted.

"Um, hello? It's Munir. Andre said I should come around this time to get the final shots."

"Come in, Munir," Nina called. "We were just leaving. I'll text Andre to come back."

CHAPTER SEVEN

THE PLANE WAS long and narrow and pointed like a pencil. It had bladed wings attached to its sides and a booster rocket as an eraser.

Nina had spent January through March living Reve's life. Staying in his secure building with its daily housekeeping and obscenely gorgeous views had already been a lifestyle far beyond her middle-class experience. He had often spoken very casually of other extravagant things, like his house in Hawaii or his yacht in Florida, so she ought to have been prepared for this.

There was a big jump between hearing him mention a supersonic jet, however, and walking into one where he was greeted with warm familiarity.

"Mr. Weston, it's nice to have you aboard." The uniformed staff placed their luggage in the stateroom located in the tail. Glancing in, Nina saw it held a king bed amid built-in furniture in glossy mahogany. The curtains were open, showing the private airfield, but the hostess touched a button that opened a skylight, allowing morning sun to pour onto the bed.

They moved into a sitting area that held a half-dozen recliners and a couple of sectionals. Everything swiveled into different configurations to allow for private conversations or conferring as a group. Tables emerged from various wall pockets for dining and holding a laptop.

Before she sat down, Nina unabashedly peeked into the galley. There was a wine fridge and something baking that smelled like fresh croissants.

She settled in a recliner that faced Reve's, and glanced behind him at the screen showing the weather and their flight plan. She was completely intimidated.

After their kiss at the showroom last night, she'd cooked dinner, wondering if something more would happen between them. The way he'd reacted after viewing her collection had been so…

Well, she didn't know what she'd seen or heard in him except that she felt as though he had finally seen her exactly as she was. There was little triumph or comfort in it, though. Especially when he skirted talking about any of it when they arrived back to the privacy of the penthouse. He knew how much he had meant to her and how deeply he'd hurt her, but he only brought up innocuous topics like how she planned to travel to Luxembourg.

Confused, she had wound up making calls to her family, bringing them up to speed on her plans. Reve had been talking to Australia when her long hours of work had caught up to her and she'd fallen into bed.

It was just a kiss, she kept telling herself. Same as she kept saying, *It was just sex*.

It was just Reve. He had this effect on her. He made her want and yearn and rationalize and wish and hope for impossible things to come true. He made her like him and laugh and want to spend every moment of her life in his presence.

But he had never wanted those sorts of roots and family ties, and she didn't understand why.

They took off, leaving a small bang behind them.

"That was it?" she asked.

"The boom? Yes. This technology has come a long way. The original was banned for overland travel because the booms were damaging buildings. They were also fuel hogs. You'll be happy to hear, we use biofuel and have a near-zero carbon emission."

This was a funny old argument they loved to dig their heels into. He called her a tree hugger who starved so she could make clothes that only rich people could buy. She called him an elite industrialist who was out of touch with the way common people really lived, even as he made off-brand car parts so blue-collar workers could save a few bucks.

They were both right *and* wrong, but she still bit.

"I imagine you're happy, too, since you live on the same planet as I do." She played with the touch screen that came out of her armrest, glancing through the various entertainment options. "This spaceship is overkill, isn't it? I mean, we're not transporting a kidney, are we?" She pretended to look under her seat for one. "Why do you need to be able to get to Paris in three-and-a-half hours?"

"Time is the new luxury, haven't you heard?" He

nodded at the air hostess to serve them breakfast. "And I like to surround myself with the very best. That's why you're in my life."

"Ha ha." She looked away, a tiny bit hurt that he would mock her like that.

The hostess efficiently made a table appear from the wall and flicked a tablecloth across it. Moments later, she brought fresh pastries with coffee and took their orders.

Nina noticed Reve was watching her as his thumb and finger rubbed pensively against the handle of his coffee mug.

"I bought this jet because I can. There was a time when I couldn't afford a baloney sandwich, even though my father somehow always had enough for a bottle. That sort of thing leaves you hungry for the rest of your life. It makes you reluctant to apologize for acquiring nice things when you can afford to buy them."

While she had known he hadn't had much growing up, she hadn't realized it was that bad. She bit her lip with contrition. "Why did you never tell me that before?"

"So you could see me as noble because I was once poor?"

"So I could understand you better."

"What's to understand? I want to eat and be warm and dry, same as everyone. I want those needs to be met consistently."

"But you don't believe they will be. Is that what you're saying?" A stark, tragic truth dawned on her.

"Deep down, you're always worried that this—" she waved at the extremely high standard of living on display "—is temporary."

"Nothing in life is permanent," he said with conviction. "But yes. That's why I have a dozen fail-safes. Property here, extra cash there. I'm like a dog burying bones in the yard." He was being very self-deprecating, and it made her ache to hear it.

For her whole life, she had always taken for granted that if her life fell apart, she could fall back on her family. In fact, she *had*. When she had walked out on Reve, she'd cried in her father's hotel room. She'd been home a few days later, sleeping in her old bed, pouring her heart out to her sister, who had helped her get back on her feet.

The one time she had worried her family wouldn't be there for her had been this recent crisis. Fearing she might lose them had been the darkest, most terrifying time of her life.

She tried to imagine a whole childhood of being that isolated and unsupported. Her throat closed on a lump.

"You don't believe people are constant, either. Do you?" she realized.

"They're not." He used his lobster fork to draw meat from the bright orange tail that had been butterflied and broiled. It sat amid deviled eggs and blanched beans decorated with capers and olives and mushrooms. "Even when people don't betray you on the way out the door, they still leave."

"Like me?" she asked in a thin voice.

"You. My PA left a couple of months ago. She worked for me for four years and I never once made her cry. I asked. She made six figures and had two months of paid vacation every year. She said it was the best job she'd ever had, but she was getting married and wanted to start a family. Now I'm training Melvin." He lifted a shoulder, conveying his lack of enthusiasm. "He's fine, but I've learned my lesson and won't get attached."

Nina broke the yolk on her poached egg so it oozed across the lox stacked with asparagus and tomato on toasted crostini. "Will you tell me what happened with *her*?"

"Her? Oh. *Her*." His mouth twisted. "It's all online. I was involved with a sex advice blogger who filmed us during an intimate moment without my knowledge. She also posted it to her site without my permission."

Nina had the feeling his lawyer had crafted that statement because it sounded word for word how he'd described it the first night they'd had dinner. *I like to get this out of the way,* he'd said. *So you understand why I am so adamant about not allowing people to use me for their personal gain.*

Since it had never been her intention to do so, and he had clearly not wanted to talk more about it, she'd pushed the whole thing to the back of her mind. He must have thought she hadn't appreciated how truly devastating it must have been.

"Would you tell me how you got together?" She was treading very carefully. "What led her to think that would be okay?"

He kept his gaze on his plate as he chewed and swallowed, then chased it with a gulp of orange juice. Just when she thought he was going to ignore her question, he spoke.

"We got together because I was twenty-two and she was a very sexually experienced twenty-nine. I was getting press for closing in on my first million. She had her blog and was determined to make her first million by thirty. She said she wanted to achieve it in her own way, without a man helping her. How ironic is *that*?"

He spoke with droll amusement but glowered into the middle distance.

"Was she angry with you?"

"Not at all. She was on a kick of trying to normalize older women sleeping with younger men. She was already writing posts about our sex life, and I didn't care because she was only using my first name. I didn't know about the video until I got a call from a reporter. I told her to take it down. She said I should enjoy the publicity and left it up. To be fair, I did benefit from it. And the publicity around the court case."

"Did she think that justified it? What happened when you went to the police?"

"They said it was her word against mine. By the time we went to court, she was claiming she'd done it to expose the lack of teeth in revenge porn laws. She came to court armed with a hundred instances where men had done something similar to women and had their cases dismissed. There was no way for her to lose at that point. Either she would become a martyr, suffering a heftier punishment than any man ever had, or our case would be dismissed like all the rest. Either way, her website was making hundreds of thousands in advertising. She made her million by thirty with months to spare," he said with false admiration.

"What happened? Was she found guilty or…?"

"She paid a fine of five hundred dollars and did thirty days of community service."

"Are you serious?"

"The laws *are* inadequate," he said with a fatalistic shrug, though she could tell he was still simmering with rage beneath his laissez-faire attitude.

"What about civil damages?"

"We settled out of court." He dipped another morsel of lobster into his melted butter. "There was no win for me in publicly flogging someone who was being lauded as a social activist for revealing a flaw in the system. I just wanted out of the spotlight. She had already received a pile of donations for her legal fund, so I had her roll it into a nonprofit that pays the fees for other victims pursuing justice for similar crimes. She is not allowed to speak my name, and whenever our tape is regurgitated into the blogosphere, I bill her for the takedown expenses."

"You must hate her so much." Nina did. She had never before wanted to cause another person harm, but she sure did now.

His expression darkened. "I'm angry with myself for allowing it to happen."

"Reve. That's called victim blaming. She did that *to* you. You didn't provoke or invite it."

"Nina." He mocked her tone of intervention. "A person like you, who has every reason to believe in others, is not to blame when someone takes your sincerely offered trust and crushes it under their heel. I already knew people could be rotten to the core. I failed to protect myself because I thought we had something."

"You loved her?" Oh, that was a dagger to the heart. Her fingers went numb. She set down her cutlery with a clatter so she wouldn't drop it.

"I don't know what I thought I felt." His cheek ticked and he didn't meet her gaze. "Whatever it was, she betrayed it in a very public and humiliating way."

She nodded jerkily. No wonder he hated paparazzi so much. She contemplated why she was going to Europe and how much attention she might garner.

"There's still time to distance yourself from me, you know. Before my identity comes out and things blow up."

"I know," he said gravely. "I will."

His quiet assertion caused her throat to close up. As she coughed and tried to recover, she realized breakfast was over for her.

Reve had offered up his heart to another woman, and she had essentially sold it to the highest bidder. Nina had no idea how to help him get past that. Why would he want to? It would mean leaving himself open to another betrayal like the one he'd already suffered. His inner walls had been forged in fire and she understood why he fought so hard to keep them in place.

Reve's phone buzzed. He pulled it out, glanced at it and said contemplatively, "Humph…" Then he set the phone facedown.

It buzzed again. Then again.

He picked it up to read the screen.

"Is something wrong?"

"Not at all." His mouth pushed sideways in something that bordered on smugness.

He started to put it down, but it buzzed again.

"Something about your deal in Berlin?"

"No," he said mildly, but when his gaze met hers, there was a light in his eyes that was pure, wicked enjoyment.

Her heart shrank, then exploded with alarm.

"You did *not* tell Andre to text you." She had expressly told the man she would be in touch if and when she wanted to know how things were going. Otherwise, he should maintain radio silence.

"I plead the Fifth." Reve set the phone facedown again and went back to eating, grinning around his fork.

She stared at his phone, not realizing she was holding her breath until it buzzed again. She gasped for air and looked at Reve.

He lifted his brows.

"Oh, for heaven's sake! *Tell me*. No, don't. Wait. Do I want to know?"

"It's not that big a deal," he said with a hitch of his shoulder, but he was shaking with quiet laughter. "You've had a bid on the unfinished gown, as is, with the sewing machine and shoes. It's from one of Andre's colleagues who designs window displays for up-scale boutiques in Asia." He reached for his phone and read, "'He set a reserve bid of twenty-five thousand dollars and has recommended a couple more buyers fly in to view the rest of your collection.'"

"No! That's…" She started to pick up her glass of orange juice but didn't trust herself. She pointed and asked the air hostess, "Can you put a little vodka in this for me, please?"

"He also has an order for the pantsuit." Reve flicked at his screen. "Only two hundred, but he's certain that will go up."

"Make it a double." She smiled heroically at the woman.

"There's been a *very* friendly tweet from *Vogue* after their sneak peek. They're teasing a full column to be posted later today. The photos are also gaining momentum on social media."

"Please stop." She set her elbows on either side of her plate, her head so dizzy she had to brace it in her hands.

"Wait." He frowned as he read. "Nina." His voice was somewhere between awe and affection. "I was already proud as hell of you, but this…?" He licked his lips, smiling with relish as he read aloud, "'Kelly Bex has requested an appointment. Per Nina's instructions, I explained that Ms. Bex has been critical of this designer's work in the past and so the designer felt there was no value in Ms. Bex attending.' *Ruthless*."

"It's true," she said with a defensive shrug, then

bit her lip. "But I also asked myself what you would do and decided she could kick rocks."

He touched his chest. "I feel like my little girl is all grown-up."

They both dissolved into laughter. The dampness in her eyes wasn't humor, though. It was more poignant than that. This was the man she'd fallen for, the one she had imagined making a life with. The closer they grew, however, the clearer the gaps between them became.

There's still time to distance yourself.

I will.

She didn't blame him for that.

But it still broke her heart.

"I've always wanted to come to Paris, and I can't explore it!" Nina lamented, her face pressed to the car window as the Eiffel Tower appeared on the far side of the Seine.

"I've booked us a private dinner cruise so you can see some of it."

"You don't have to do that." She sat back.

"It's done." He brushed it aside. "We both have to eat. I never take time to enjoy the city when I'm here." And he wanted to make the most of the little time they had.

There's still time to distance yourself.

He became perversely annoyed every time she said something like that. He could take care of himself. She was the one he was worried about, thinking she could put on a pair of sunglasses and wander around like Sherlock Holmes looking for clues.

They left the river and headed into the Eighth Arrondissement.

"That's Oriel's building," he said as they approached it. He recognized it from the street view online. "The yellow one."

Nina sat up, alert. "She's not there. She's in Mumbai. They had dinner with her husband's sister last night—which you would know if you went anywhere near a gossip site." She swung her head around to flash him a teasing smile. "Their photos are everywhere."

She leaned to look upward against the window as they passed the building.

"Oh, shoot." She quickly slouched into her seat again. "I think there was a photographer waiting for her on the stoop. He jumped to his feet when he saw me." She craned to look out the rear window. "He might be following us. I'm really sorry."

He shrugged. "We're catching the train in the morning."

"To Luxembourg? You're coming with me?"

"I am." He might not read gossip sites, but he had devoted some time to reading up on Oriel. The model was being mobbed everywhere she went.

That sort of attention might be bearable if there was a visible endpoint, the way interest died down after a court case was settled. Oriel was expecting, though. Each detail of her pregnancy was being picked apart and, if history was anything to go by, the world had an endless appetite for celebrity babies. There was also speculation that Lakshmi's manager had forced her to give up her baby, and the mystery of Oriel's biological father had yet to be solved.

Given all of that, Lakshmi's story was destined to make headlines forever. Once Nina came forward, the publicity would explode exponentially.

Reve had no desire to be in the middle of that, not only because he loathed the idea of his own scandal being dredged up. He was never happy when that happened, but he'd learned to live with it. No, he was dreading his history smearing Nina. She had enough to deal with.

He couldn't bring himself to let her face all of this alone, though. Better to help her fly under the radar a little longer and enjoy her last few days of anonymity.

His driver turned onto Avenue Montaigne and stopped outside his building. They hurried inside before any scooters caught up and, moments later, entered a space that seamlessly mixed old-world authenticity with modern expectations. The attic space above his unit had been opened to the main floor, creating high ceilings and skylights that allowed light to pour down to the living space on the main floor.

A wine and a charcuterie board awaited them. Nina ignored the pinwheel of meats, cheeses, fruit, crackers, nuts and olives, instead swinging wide the doors to the narrow terrace that ran the length of the apartment. She plucked a sprig from an herb plant in the pot and rubbed it between her palms, inhaling the fragrance before sighing as she looked out at the cityscape.

"I'm starting to think it would be worth the notoriety if it meant I could walk into the boutiques I've dreamed of seeing my whole life," she said with a wistful sigh.

"Come." He took her hand and tugged her back into the apartment.

He felt the jolt go through her. It sent a spark of electricity straight into his groin.

He was leading her toward a bedroom for other reasons, but the way her lips parted and her expression grew soft and receptive nearly fried all of his best intentions.

"It might take you some time to dress for dinner." His voice wasn't quite even. "You should get started picking out your clothes."

"Why? If it's a private cruise, I can go like this, can't—? Oh, *Reve*."

She stepped into the spare bedroom where the bed had been removed and racks brought in from a dozen of the most exclusive haute couture designers. Not the dominant names exported worldwide, but the up-and-comers who had moved to Paris from Tokyo, Seoul, Saint Petersburg and São Paulo.

She sagged into him as though confronting something too monumental to face. Her fist closed on his shirtfront while she stared and stared.

"What have you done? That's seven figures. Easily."

"I don't expect you to keep *all* of them."

The look on her face was worth every penny if she did, though. Her mouth trembled and her eyes gleamed. There was awe and excitement, anticipation and reverence.

It disappeared as she turned her face into the crook of his neck, hugging him so hard she shook with it.

Reve had never had Christmas as a child. As an adult, he went through the motions of bonuses and corporate gifts because it was expected, not because he really understood the celebration. It sounded a lot like doing someone else's shopping and then lying about it. Santa was, at best, a manipulation tactic. At worst, he was a cruelty against less fortunate children who were striving to be "good" for a promise that wouldn't manifest.

This was it, though. This was Christmas—giving someone something they had always wanted. Taking Nina by surprise and witnessing pure joy on her face was filling his chest with a swell of pride and pleasure and a sense that they now shared something deeply personal and precious.

He could hardly breathe as he prompted her to go into the room. "Don't you want to meet your new friends?"

She was still shaking. She was *crying*.

His heart lurched.

"Nina. I thought you would like this."

"I do. I'm so excited I can't bear it." She drew back and pushed the heel of her shaking hand across her cheek. "But I don't want to lose myself in that because…" She looked up at him and her chin trembled.

She wiped another track of tears from her other cheek. "Because it takes away from my time with you. I want to be with you, Reve. Like, *with* you. I know it's not forever, but for what little time we have."

She played with the button on his shirt, and his libido resounded like a struck gong, singing *yes!*

Then a harder, crueler sensation pierced into his stomach.

"That's not what this is, Nina." He dropped his arms from around her and stepped back. "I'm not trying to bribe you into sleeping with me."

CHAPTER EIGHT

"THAT'S NOT WHAT I think." She caught his hand as he started to move away. "Not anymore. But you've done *so much* for me—"

"I'm not interested in being paid back for any of that," he said coldly.

"That's not what I'm trying to do!" She let go of his hand and they glared at each other.

She folded her arms and looked at the clothes.

"You did nice things for me before, and I thought it meant you cared, really cared. And I built that into all these big assumptions based on what I'd always imagined I would have when I found the right man. When I realized… When I realized you didn't love me, I thought all of those things you'd done were—"

"I know what you thought," he said through his teeth. His profile was hard as hammered iron.

"I hated myself for being so blind, for wasting my time, *myself*, with someone so shallow."

She heard his sharp inhale.

"But that's not what you are," she hurried to say, taking a step toward him. "And I realize now why you don't have the same expectations I do. I respect that. You're still a good person."

He snorted. "No, I'm not. And the more I learn about you, the more I realize what a bastard I was for getting involved with you. I didn't mean to lead you on, but I did. If anything, this is me trying to buy your good opinion." He waved at the clothes.

"It's working."

He swore under his breath and rejected that with a jerk of his head.

"It's true," she insisted. "I needed to know that I wasn't completely blind, Reve. That you really are generous and protective and thoughtful and have a core of integrity. I needed to know the man I fell for wasn't a mirage."

"But I *am*," he assured her.

"No, you're not." She set her hand on the front of his shirt and let her fingernails slip between the buttons so her touch sat against his warm skin.

"Don't." He caught her wrist.

Beneath his tense expression she saw a flash of something that might have been stark need.

"Don't do this," he said in a roughened voice that might have been an order or a plea. "Because I will take you to bed and I will hurt you again. Not because I want to, but because I can't be the man you want. It wouldn't be fair to you."

"Really, Reve? Talk to me about how fair life is." Her voice creaked. The things he'd told her on the plane were still sitting inside her, jagged as broken glass. "Life is *never* as simple as we want it to be.

Even a dream as common as marriage and family is harder to achieve that it sounds. Look at my dad, losing the love of his life far too young. My sister, unable to carry the baby she desperately wants."

"Exactly why I won't risk falling in love! I don't want to expect good things and have them turn bad."

"I don't expect you to fall in love. I don't expect anything from you if we have sex." She dipped her head against his chest. "I shouldn't have expected anything before."

His hands came to her shoulders as if to push her away, yet there was no force in them. They rested there while tension gripped him.

She lifted her gaze to his hungry, indecisive expression.

Slowly she let her body lean into his. Tiny detonations began going off inside her as his warmth seeped through their clothing, past her skin and into her blood. Her throat and breasts and belly and thighs grew hot. She touched her mouth under his chin.

His chest expanded and his hands shifted up her back.

"I am only a man, you know." His voice reverberated against her lips where she touched them next to his Adam's apple. "And this is all I've been thinking about."

"Me, too."

He choked a laugh, already dropping his head, sealing their mouths together.

The intensity of sensation that went through her might have alarmed her if his strong arms hadn't closed around her, grounding her. Promising to keep her safe.

She curled her arms around his neck and conveyed that he should kiss her harder, but he skated his mouth across her cheek to her ear and whispered, "Slowly."

His lips nibbled around the shell of her ear, his breath tickling until the hair on her scalp and arms stood up. Her knees softened and she gasped, "I don't think I can wait."

"You will have to, though, won't you?" His tongue dabbled at her earlobe. "Because I will not squander this time, Nina. Not one second of it."

What had she unleashed? A beast. A possessive, patient, tender, sensual beast. His arms tightening, his mouth went to her throat, and her nipples stung where they pressed against his chest.

"Reve." She roamed her hands over his flexing shoulders, standing on tiptoe and tilting her head so he could bite softly at the tendon where her neck joined her shoulder. He was hard. She could feel him against her mound. She was excited, but she wanted to savor this, too. She brought his mouth back to hers, and they shared a long, lazy, powerful kiss that became her entire existence.

When she drew back, she blinked with incomprehension, surprised to find herself here, with him, in Paris.

Lust shone from between his tangled lashes. He turned her and walked with himself glued to her back, ambling slowly and kissing her neck as he guided her into the master bedroom.

"I've always liked this dress on you," he said, sliding his hands over the brushed jersey against her stomach.

"Why? Because it's soft?" The wrap dress was comfortable and the mauve color flattering to her skin tone. She'd put it on for travel thinking if she *was* spotted, at least she would be wearing one of her own designs.

"Because it's sexy as hell. Short and flirty." His hand traced along the belt to fiddle with the tails of the bow that draped her hip and then followed to where the skirt flap overlapped. "You think I haven't been staring at your legs all day?"

"These old things? They barely run."

"Hmm. Funny." She felt his smile against her nape.

The floor in the bedroom was parquet wood in a basket weave pattern. She lifted her gaze to a fireplace that looked through to a bathtub. There was a painting above it in silver and blue abstract ribbons. The massive bed was made up with white and gray bedding, and a translucent white curtain covered the pair of doors onto the terrace.

"This is beautiful." Romantic. Like a dream. A perfect fantasy, which was all this was.

He said, "I can't see anything but you," and she was okay with fantasy.

She sent him a look over her shoulder.

He kissed her smile away, then said, "Before I get too distracted…" He went to the night table, withdrew a box of condoms from the drawer and turned it to find the expiration date. "Still good." He left them next to the lamp.

She had noticed he'd used one the other day, and even though a small pang of hurt had struck, she admonished herself that *she* had left *him*.

"What's wrong?" He came across and stilled the hands she was wringing, forcing her to lift her gaze to his.

"Nothing."

"Nina. We can't do this if we're not going to be honest with each other."

"It's fine that you've been with other people," she blurted. "I didn't expect any different."

"I haven't been with anyone." His head went back. "I used a condom the other day because I thought you might have been with someone. Maybe that boyfriend you left when you came to New York?"

"He's married now."

She wasn't sure of the wave of stiff emotion encasing him, but she thought it might be defensiveness. Did he think it said something about how important she'd been to him that he hadn't found anyone else?

Don't, Nina. She needed to keep this in perspective.

She brushed away deeper yearnings and offered a saucy smile. "Put those straight back in the drawer."

One side of his mouth pulled. "You think you're in charge here? Think again."

She grew tight all over, anticipation overwhelming her. She wanted him to drag her dress apart and ravage her, but he only picked up the tail of her braid where it dangled in front of her shoulder.

"I've been staring at this all day, too. Thinking about taking it apart." He removed the elastic from the end. His gaze came up to crash into hers. "Thinking about taking you apart."

Excited tension rose in her throat. If she were another animal, it might have been a purr or a growl.

He took his time, the rogue, working his fingers into her braid to free it, turning her so he could follow it when it turned into a French braid that started above her opposite ear. He paused a few times to set maddening kisses against her neck.

"I like the pink." He turned her to face him and combed his fingers into her hair. "I want to feel you run this all over my naked skin."

"Oh, you think you're in charge?"

"I do." He made one careful revolution of the hand still tangled in her hair. Now he had her trapped with a tighter grip. "I think you're at my mercy." He touched his mouth to her lips, barely leaving a burning spark of static before he set a peck on her nose and a tender kiss on her brow. Another grazed her cheekbone, then the corner of her mouth, then the base of her throat.

He roamed his free hand all over her, waking her body to his touch. She did the same, rediscovering the muscled strength beneath his crisp shirt and tailored trousers.

When she felt the belt of her dress tugged open, she held her breath. A cool rush of air wafted across her abdomen and upper thighs as he opened the dress. His hot hand crept inside, sliding across her waist and around to her lower back, drawing her half-naked body into his clothed one. The cool metal of his belt buckle branded her stomach.

"Reve." She curled one hand under his arm to rest on his shoulder blade, her other around his neck.

"Why have I never taken you dancing, Nina?" His hand went to her tailbone, but he left the other in her hair. He opened his hot mouth against her neck as he gently swayed them against one another.

Her mind nearly exploded, she was accosted by so many sensations. Her hands moved on him, trying to ground herself in his solidness, but her eyes nearly rolled into the back of her head as he continued placing seductive kisses across her collarbone and under her chin.

When he kissed her again, the tenderness was still there, but the heat had arrived. The *need*.

But even as she drank up his deep, ravenous kisses and sucked flagrantly on his bottom lip, sinking ever deeper into the greedy underworld of lust, she was overwhelmed with a tremendous need to *give*.

His hand slid down to her bottom, palming her cheek through lace and silk, and she moved in time with his petting, seeking more of his fondling while also pressing into the hardness behind his fly. When she would have dipped her mouth into his throat, the sharp tug against her scalp reminded her he still had a fistful of her hair.

They looked at each other with dazed eyes. He released her, causing her to wince a little as he untangled his fingers, but he smoothed his hand over her hair in apology and wordlessly drew her back into their kiss.

Now they blatantly tangled their tongues and clung to each other, and her only thought was that she didn't know how she had lived without him. Without this. She wanted to stand on his feet and climb inside him. Have nothing between them but the perspiration he brought forth onto her skin.

He drew back enough to brush her dress off her shoulders, his gaze reverent as he looked down on her breasts. She opened the front closure of her bra herself, peeling back the cups in offering, reveling in the growling noise that sounded in his throat as he cupped her breasts, firmly and slowly, massaging as he went back to kissing her, then finding her nipples and giving gentle pinches that struck twin shots of electric gold straight to her loins.

A sob escaped her and she gave a light scrape of her nails through his shirt against his shoulders, telling him how torturous this was.

When he let her breathe, she gasped, "I can't stand. I'm too weak."

"I'll hold you up." He wrapped his arms around her, his hands going to her bottom again, sliding inside her panties and squeezing the taut globes.

She stood on tiptoe, barefoot because she'd kicked off her sandals when she entered the apartment. She clung to him and felt all of her inhibitions slipping away. Everything in her became *want*. His.

She rubbed him through his pants and felt his whole body go taut. "Do you want my mouth here?"

"Yes." His breath hissed through his teeth as she continued caressing him. "Your hands, your mouth. I want to suck your nipples until you're ready to come. I want to feel your thighs squeezing my ears when you do."

She was nearly there now, her panties so damp he must feel it where he was reaching his long finger from the back of her thigh toward her hot core.

"What are you waiting for?" She sucked the side of his neck, wanting to mark him. Wishing she had the right to call him hers for all time.

His muscles gathered and he twisted, pressing her toward the bed. She sat and opened her knees, hooking her hands in his belt to draw him closer. It was the playful push-pull they'd always had. The small oversteps of familiarity formed a link of trust that grew stronger with each passionate encounter.

As she began to unbuckle him, however, it struck her this might be one of the last times she made love with him. It made her clumsy as she worked to open his fly and push his pants off his hips.

She exposed his thick, straining erection, and his hands on her shoulders gave a restrained clench while she breathed out a shaken breath upon him. His abdomen hollowed and she kissed the tense muscles there. Then she tasted and caressed and swallowed him into her mouth, applying delicate suction so his hands moved to her head and he shook.

His breaths were the sound of metal on gravel, uneven and loud enough to fill the room. His buttocks were hard. She tested them with the sharp dig of her fingernails and wanted to finish him like this. Leave a memory in him that would live eternally, but he dragged himself free of the draw of her lips and clenched his fist around his shaft, visibly straining to keep control of himself.

"My turn." He set splayed fingertips on her chest and nudged her to fall backward onto the mattress, then leaned over her to kiss her.

He ravaged her mouth the way she'd been aching for him to do. The way that said she was his entire world right now, the only thing that mattered to him. His bare chest was against hers, the fine hairs just rough enough when she twisted to create delicious friction. His steely thighs were planted between her twitching legs. His hot sex teased her through the wet silk of her panties.

She ran her hands under the edges of his open shirt, caressing his damp back, and pushed the shirt off his shoulders. He lifted long enough to throw it away, then gathered her breasts again, murmuring, "So pretty."

His mouth went to her collarbone, her breastbone, the upper swell of her chest and the turgid nipple of one breast. He tortured the other with a soft pinch, keeping it up as she wriggled and dove her hands into his hair and tried to speak past the swirl of intense pleasure that gripped her.

He shifted and his blunt tip pressed against her, teasingly blocked by wet silk.

"Move it," she gasped, trying to grapple the placket aside.

"I want all of you." He went to his knees, as aware as she was that their time was short. That they couldn't hold anything back at this point because there wouldn't be a next time.

That thought had her giving herself over to him, letting him kiss and lick at the insides of her thighs and steal her panties.

His bared teeth were too feral to be called a smile as he easily arranged her how he wanted her, with her thighs draped over his upper arms. His breath wafted against her curls.

"Hello, lovely." He parted her and swept his tongue along her folds, slowly tightening the coil of need in her abdomen with ruthless languor.

When she gasped, "I want you inside me," and tugged at his hair, he slid a finger inside her and continued lapping and loving and driving her ever closer to sheer madness. She trembled with need, moaning with loss as he removed his finger. Two came back, and he delicately worked them in and out of her as he swirled and sucked.

Her last vestige of self-consciousness disappeared and she became pure instinct. She pressed him to increase his tempo and lifted her hips into the press of his mouth. Then she gave herself up to the wild wave that threw her into the abyss.

She might have screamed. She didn't know.

This. Reve needed nothing in life beyond Nina exactly like this, utterly weak with passion. He kicked off his pants and shifted her into the middle of the bed, then settled over her. His swollen tip felt as though he would split his skin, but he soothed the ache by anointing himself against her slippery, pulsing folds.

She made a soft, receptive noise and her knee came up, her calf slipping across his back with invitation.

He slid in and went blind at the sensation—hot and soft and blissfully wet. She was the only woman he had ever been truly naked with, which wasn't the only reason this was so intensely pleasurable. It was the surrender in her soft body beneath his, the welcome in her sigh against his ear. The heaviness in her eyelids and the caress of her fingertips against his spine reduced the world to just this. Them. Joined.

He had forgotten how profound this was, and his heart shook in warning.

He might have withdrawn then, but the slightest friction on his impatient flesh sizzled his brain and caused her to hum with renewed arousal. He felt a quake of pleasure go through her and he was lost.

His only thought then was to hold back while he waited for her to catch up to him. He made himself lie still with his heartbeat buried inside her. When he whispered how good she felt around him, she shivered and tightened her clasp on his flesh.

He caressed her shoulders and arms and thighs and bottom, sliding his touch to where they were joined, and delicately drew another hum of awareness from her. He contorted so he could suckle her nipples and feel the lovely tension gather in her.

When she opened her eyes and he saw the haze

of passion clouding her pretty brown eyes, he rolled her to straddle him.

This was the woman who had haunted him for months. She sat tall and ran her hands over herself, watching him with a seductive smile as she touched where she held him captive.

He ground his teeth and cupped her breasts, lifting his hips because he was unable to help himself.

Her pupils seemed to explode. She caught his wrists and began to lift and roll as she rode him. Every breath was a harsh sob that accompanied the impact of their flesh. He moved his hands to her hips, guiding her so they were in perfect sync.

Her sobs grew more anxious as she closed in on the finish. His throat burned with the ragged noises he was making, striving to hang on, to get there, to arrive at exactly the same moment—

She froze, and her mouth hung open to release a silent scream.

All his senses disappeared. He was torn from this world for long seconds before he was thrown back with such a slam of pleasure, it was nearly pain. He gripped her hips, trying to meld them into one as he bucked with jolts of sheer ecstasy.

He knew at a distance that he was losing something of himself. Something he would never get back. But in these sharp, endless, euphoric seconds, he didn't give one tiny damn.

She could have all of him. He was already hers.

CHAPTER NINE

"For a four-hour train trip?" Nina looked around the extravagant stateroom that was their private car. "This looks like something from the Orient Express." She trailed her fingertips along the beveled edge of the cherrywood dining table, wondering what he must have paid to have this car added since she doubted this route typically had sleeper cars.

"I tried to book a helicopter. You said no." He hung his jacket in the closet.

"Because I thought I would be traveling alone and would buy the ticket myself." When he'd asked her in New York how she wanted to travel to Luxembourg, she had thought he was making conversation, trying to avoid talking about their kiss at the showroom. "I wanted to go by train so I could watch the scenery." She peeked through the closed drapes.

"We'll open them once we get going. At least in here, we don't have to see anyone, not even the conductor. Unless there's something we don't have." He glanced in the well-stocked refrigerator and checked the labels on the wine in the racks. "Hungry?"

"We just had breakfast." She glanced around the jut of a separation wall. The top of it was clouded by etched glass, and the bottom was cherrywood paneling that matched the rest of the room. There was a very plush-looking double bed tucked behind it.

"We could go back to bed," she suggested.

They had been doing little else other than making love since last night. Dinner on the Seine had been canceled, and they'd made do with the charcuterie board for dinner. They had wound up fooling around on a dining room chair and then having sex on the sofa. They'd dozed there, then had a bath together— along with a couple of orgasms. Sometime after midnight, they'd woken and come together in a wordless fog of simply needing to be joined.

They'd both risen achy and sore this morning, agreeing that it had to stop. But they'd showered together and landed on the sheets soaking wet, groaning each other's names as they drove each other to another lofty pinnacle.

It was the best possible madness, and also a type of hoarding for the cold winter they were both avoiding any mention of.

"You're not going to see much from the bed," Reve chided, his eyelids already drooping with the drug of lust.

Nina lifted her chin. "Depends what I want to see, doesn't it? For instance, I have had it with that tie." She pointed. "Get rid of it."

"I pity the conductor," he said as he loosened the red silk with its subtle paisley pattern. "Having to go home to his wife and tell her he found a couple today who had literally screwed themselves to death."

"We all die of something. Pick your poison."

He barked a laugh. "You. It has to be you." He tackled her in a handful of steps, tumbling her onto the bed beneath him.

This immersion in each other was pure denial of reality, as well as deliriously exquisite.

Also, it turned out to be exactly what they needed. They conked out immediately after climaxing and jerked awake when a bell sounded. A voice announced, "Arriving at your destination in fifteen minutes."

"Is this one of those hibernation capsules, and we've traveled through space and time?" She rose to dress, her brain barely functioning. "I am definitely not going to earn the fashion designer's secret handshake if they see the way I treat my new clothes."

She shook out her chiffon culottes—an old standby that a Tokyo designer had given a chic makeover. They hugged her waist and hips then fell in loose, flirty pleats to accentuate her calves and ankles. Her muslin blouse by a Vancouver designer was a deceptively simple peasant style that had its own billowy grace.

When she'd gone through her things from Reve's storage, she'd found and reclaimed her lace-up retro-looking saddle shoes. They'd served her well on the endless sidewalk commutes of New York so she'd brought them for what she expected would be a lot of footwork in the tiny village near Mondorf-les-Bains.

The spa town had sprung up around the discovery of a hot spring back in the eighteen hundreds, but a smaller, more exclusive "retreat" had been built among the neighboring vineyards a hundred years later. It hadn't had thermal waters, but it did have top doctors charging top dollar for discreet services.

As the train slowed, she glanced up from fixing her hair to see Reve watching her with a sober expression as he knotted his tie. Each rock of the carriage was a slow tick of their time winding down. They both felt it.

"Don't look like that." He came over to squeeze her shoulder and kiss the top of her head. "Nothing in life stays the same."

He was right, but it still put a lump in her throat.

She donned sunglasses and a hat, but if there had been any interest in Oriel's connection to Luxembourg, it was long over. No one seemed to give them a second glance as they disembarked. A young man waited with a key fob and directed them to a sedan outside the train station.

Reve programmed their destination into the navigation system, and within minutes they were traveling east toward the German border, leaving the city for softly rolling hills and picturesque villages.

"Was there no border check when your mother came through?" Reve asked as the Moselle River came into view. "Did she realize she was leaving Germany?"

"It was already a very low-key system. She stopped to ask the border guard where they could eat while she figured out how to get back to where they were going. He suggested the café where she wound up collapsing."

"The investigator said there were private houses in the area that were a cottage industry—pun intended. They provided discreet accommodation for the celebs who used the clinic, but he wasn't able to find which one Lakshmi stayed at. Most of them are still operating, serving the wine tour crowd."

"Is that where we're staying?"

"Actually, he found a vineyard owned by the family of the doctor who signed your birth certificate. I had to pay triple to get another reservation bumped, but I'm hoping to succeed where the investigator failed. Get some answers."

"That's a lot of money for them to take one look at me and refuse to say anything without a lawyer present." Her stomach was nothing but snakes and butterflies as the car ate up the miles.

"We'll see."

"Are you enjoying this?" she asked, narrowing her eyes in suspicion.

"A little." He side-eyed her. "It's a puzzle. I'm curious. And I want you to have answers." He reached to squeeze her hand.

That sounded a little like he was emotionally invested, but she didn't tease him over it. She let the sparks of possibility dance in her, even though she knew it was an indulgence she couldn't afford.

A short while later, they stepped from the car in front of a villa surrounded by rows upon rows of grapevines. A dog wagged itself nearly to pieces as it waddled up to them.

A middle-aged woman came out of a stone cottage nearby. She was wiping her hands on a tea towel. Her smile fell away into shock.

"When they said a high-profile couple from New York insisted on staying here, I didn't realize…" The woman gave Reve a confused look, perhaps expecting Oriel's Indian husband, before mustering a fresh smile for them both. "I'm Farrah. Let me show you into the house. My husband, Charles, will bring your luggage if you'd like to give me the key to the car."

"Reve Weston. And—"

"I know who you are." Farrah flipped her tea towel onto her shoulder.

Reve left it at that and said, "We're hoping to speak to the doctor's family. Are you…?"

"No relation." Farrah shook her head. "Charles and I arrived ten years ago. Answered an ad. The family needed someone to run things because the doctor had passed away and he was the one with the passion for the vineyard."

"Dr. Wagner?" Nina cocked her head. "The one who worked at the clinic?"

"That's what I was told. Like I say, before our time, but I understand he came from Austria every week or so and had all sorts of famous clients." Farrah opened the door into the villa. "His family still lives in Austria. I run this as a vacation rental. Charles manages the vineyard."

Inside, the house was bright and well maintained if

slightly dated. It had a beautiful terrace with expansive views of the vineyard and the silver river below.

Charles came in with their luggage and Reve asked him to leave it by the door. He took back the key and they drove straight into the village. The investigator hadn't had much luck at the café, but Reve went in while Nina stayed in the car, sunglasses on like an undercover cop on stakeout.

Reve came back with pastries and the news. "The owner will ask his father if he remembers a pregnant American woman collapsing twenty-five years ago, but the old man's memory is failing. We shouldn't expect too much. I left him my card."

"Humph."

They tried the small medical clinic that serviced the village. The receptionist had no desire to tell anyone the names of any retired medical professionals living in the area. Then they drove to the spa, which was swarming with tourists and didn't inspire Nina to believe there was much they could learn there, either.

They returned to the vineyard and took a walk to stretch their legs and breathe the warm, earth-flavored air, but she was feeling very disheartened.

"It was a waste of time to come all this way, wasn't it?" Not to mention the cost to him.

"You wanted to know what you could find. Now you do. Did you expect it all to become crystal clear the second we arrived?"

"Kind of," she said glumly.

"Come here." He drew her into his embrace.

It felt so natural to be with him like this, leaning

on him and lifting her mouth for the kiss he lingered over. How could this be anything other than the way they were meant to be?

"Where do we go from here?" she asked with a forlorn pang in her throat.

"I'll call Oriel's husband if you want." His hands roamed her back, but his touch didn't soothe the prickles of anguish gathering within her.

"I can do that." She drew back. "And once I do… Where do *we* go?"

He dragged in a pained breath, and he gripped her arms briefly before setting her away from him. "This is what I was trying to avoid," he muttered.

"I *know*. And I'm not blaming you or trying to pressure you into anything, but I don't want to say goodbye, Reve. I…" She clutched at her elbows, feeling hollow inside. "I feel safe with you."

He swore under his breath and ran his hand through his hair. "I don't. I feel as though I'm losing every part of myself when I'm with you, and that's terrifying."

His words set fire to her chest.

Whatever anguish came into her face made him wince and turned away.

"I can't be like you. Open and trusting."

"Because of her." She meant the woman who had posted his sex tape.

"Her, my father, my aunt. Anytime I've let myself believe in others they have always let me down."

"What happened with your aunt?"

"Nothing," he said flatly, his profile sharp as

chipped granite. He squinted as he looked to the past, and his voice grew raspy. "She turned up looking just like the photo I had of my mother. I remember this shred of hope coming awake inside me. I thought, *Now things will get better.*" His face contorted with helpless anger. "But she looked around and asked my father, 'How can you live like this?' and left me there."

His bitterness was so tangible she tasted it on her own tongue. She felt his crushing disappointment as a profound weight on her chest.

"And then I left," she said with anguish, hating herself for doing that to him.

"What were you going to stay for?" he asked with self-disgust. "*I* broke what we had. You're right about that. I *am* broken."

"Reve, don't." She started toward him, but he stiffened in rejection and she halted. "You're not. I never should have said that. I was being cruel because I was hurt."

"It's still true. I'll never be able to give you what you want, Nina. I could go through the motions. Marry you and give you kids, but you want more than a couple of boxes ticked. You want things inside me that just aren't there."

"I don't know what I want anymore," she cried, unable to imagine finding happiness with someone else when the price was him.

"You do." He rounded on her. "You want the kind of love you've always known. I won't let you compromise yourself and settle for less because we happen to be good in bed."

His voice was so harsh and final that her mouth began to quiver. She couldn't stand here and start bawling like a child.

"I'm going to run a bath," she choked, and hurried inside.

CHAPTER TEN

HER VISION WAS so blurred by the onset of tears that she tripped over their suitcases, still in the foyer.

She cursed loudly and bitterly as she went down. The floor jarred her palm and her knee crashed onto the stone tiles. For a brief second, she sat there stunned by the lightning-sharp agony of her fall as it outshone the despair overwhelming her.

Reve lurched in behind her. "What happened? Are you okay?" He swore when he saw her trying to pick herself up amid their tumbled bags. "That's my fault. I told him to leave them there."

"Don't worry about it."

When he tried to help her, she recoiled, unable to let him touch her right now. She would fall apart for sure.

A grim silence formed around him as he picked up both their bags and started up the stairs.

She followed to the master bedroom, afraid to so much as thank him because she was on the brink of a breakdown.

Before she had properly taken in the luxurious

room in cream and moss tones, Reve slipped around her and walked out—with his own case in his hand.

Reve. His name stayed locked in her throat, hot and sharp. He wouldn't even sleep with her.

Biting her lip, she took slow, deliberate breaths, telling herself she would wait until she was in the tub, but agony was gushing upward within her, filling her with greater and greater swathes of misery. She was sniffling and gasping, going through the motions of opening the taps and waiting for the water to warm, trying not to hate herself for being honest with him. She only wished—

Reve walked in.

"Do you ever knock?" she cried, and swiped guiltily at her wet cheeks. Through her dejection, a streak of hope flashed to life.

His hard expression became even more severe. He moved around her to turn off the water. "I have to show you something."

His voice was grim, and her blood went cold in her veins.

Dread became a heavy boulder atop the emotions that were sitting under the surface of her control. Leaving the drip of the tap behind, she followed him from the master bedroom to the end of the upper hall. His suitcase stood outside the door of a spare bedroom as far from the master as possible.

Okay, I get it. You regret ever meeting me.

He pointed into the room. "Look."

She peered through the open doorway. It wasn't a bedroom. It was a den with a sofa that she imagined pulled out into a bed. There were floor-to-ceiling shelves stuffed with books and board games and DVDs. In one corner sat a wooden desk with a globe and an old-fashioned-looking landline telephone. On the other wall, a television sat on a credenza. A gaming console was hooked up to it, and the controllers were on the coffee table.

"What?" She moved to glance out the window. It was the uphill view of the vineyard, pretty but nothing she hadn't seen already.

"Look." He followed her in and lifted the crocheted tablecloth that served as a doily on the credenza. "Twelve drawers. What do you want to bet these little cardholders once held labels that went A/B, C/D, E/F…?"

"Oh, my God." She began yanking at the pulls, running the alphabet as she did. "K/L— They're all locked."

"It's full, though." He grabbed an end, and the tendons in his neck and arms strained as he tried to lift it. He gave it a push, but it was solid as a rock. "They haven't painted behind it. This has been here for years."

"You don't think it holds the doctor's records. Not *here*. Not *still*."

"Why not? Say you're a doctor traveling from Austria to treat private patients. Where would you store their records?"

"At the clinic."

"Until they're discharged, sure. After that, it's risky to leave them there with staff and other patients coming and going. No sense dragging them back and forth to Austria. Maybe you get a couple of your burliest laborers to drag this behemoth up to your home office and store them here. When you die, no one bothers to clean it out because it's locked and this is just a spare room where the kids play video games."

"Where's the key? On a keychain in Austria?" She moved to the desk and started rummaging through the drawers, finding only crayons and coloring books.

"Is there a letter opener?" Reve ran his hand around the edges of the credenza, then lifted the doily to expose the lock mechanism. "This will take about five seconds to pop."

"We can't break in."

"What's the difference between that and unlocking it with a key?"

"Good point. We should contact the family and ask for permission to search it. Otherwise, we might invade the privacy of living and dead celebrities." She stared at the cabinet with equal measures of temptation and regret.

"That's exactly why I think it still holds the doctor's records. It's a solid asset for a family to hold on to."

"Reve! That is by far the most cynical thing you have ever said. We don't know anything about this family. Do you really think they would keep something like this as an insurance policy? So they could bribe a dead doctor's patients if they ran out of money?"

"*Yes*. Nina—" He stared at her as he gave his head

a bemused shake. "The more I realize how naive you really are, the more I realize how badly I took advantage of you. This entire property is a laundry for the doctor's side hustle with celebrity patients. Do you not see that?"

"You don't know that. You're just guessing." As she said it, she felt the sting of truth. They were here because her birth had been covered up by this doctor. It stood to reason that more than one crime had been committed over the years. She folded her arms, saying defensively, "I like to give people the benefit of the doubt."

"Me, for instance. I always thought you were blowing smoke when you complimented me, being sweet so I'd let you stay in my home. Turns out you're actually that innocent and charming. I'm not."

"What are you doing?" Nina asked as Reve moved into the hall to open his suitcase.

"Criming." He found his nail clippers and clicked the file open like a jackknife. He would never be the kind of man she wanted or deserved, but at least he could help her unlock the secrets of her past. "If you prefer not to be implicated, I suggest you leave."

He tried to slide the file into the mechanism and discovered it was seized from lack of use. Might need oil, so he crouched to see if he could slide the file along the crack and release the mechanism that way.

"How do you know how to do that?"

"Do you really want to know?"

She was still hugging herself, her shoulders hunched. "Yes."

His chest felt constricted by coils of thick rope that were sliding and burning across his naked skin.

I don't know what I want anymore.

She didn't want him. He knew that much. She only thought she did because he'd hidden the worst of himself from her. It was time she understood why it was best they stop their involvement and part for good.

"I used to break into cars."

"For money?"

"Kind of. I learned to do it at the junkyard where I grew up, so I could strip parts and sell them to local shops. Then a couple of men from those shops started asking me to break into cars on the street. They would say it was their uncle's car or it belonged to a customer. When I was picked up by the police, I realized I was being used to take the initial risk. They stole them once the car was open. That's when I learned that innocent people get used so it's best to keep my eyes open."

"How old were you?" she asked with astonishment.

"Eleven." The nail file wasn't strong enough to jimmy the latch. He went back to his bag for his lip balm and lubricated the file, returning to work on picking the lock. "While I was at middle school, I realized I could use the library computer to set up websites and sell parts that way."

"That's how you got started as an auto parts dealer."

"That's what my PR prints in my bio, yeah." He

wiggled the file in the lock, trying to work the waxiness of the lip balm against the pins so they'd move. "But stripping parts is sweaty, time-consuming work, and shipping them is a pain in the ass. I realized I could simply become a broker, match seller with buyer and take a cut of the transaction. Fill the site full of ads and make money that way, too."

"I'm impressed that you thought to do that so young, but it doesn't sound bad. Agents are allowed to take a cut for a service they offer."

"The parts were hot, Nina. That sort of agent is called a *fence*."

"Oh." Her eyes widened.

So naive. He had always thought that was an act, and now he saw how real her trust was. It made him sick that he had walked all over her, soaking up her softness and passion as if he had a right to it. That's why this had to stop. He knew how mismatched they were and, he was realizing, she wasn't tough enough to protect herself. Not against him. He had to do that for her.

"Are you still, um…?" Her brows were squiggled with perplexity as she tried to figure out if she had been sleeping with an active criminal all this time.

"I mostly stick to the rules these days, but that's how I know a laundry when I see one. When my dad died, I was sixteen. I closed my site and used the money I'd made to buy a run-down repair shop in Detroit. If anyone asked, I said my inheritance paid for it, but my father hadn't owned the land we squatted on. I left town owing for his cremation. I'm actually not much of a mechanic, but I knew how to get good parts for cheap, and that was most of my business."

"Were the parts still hot?"

"Mostly aftermarket knockoffs unless it was a special case. I knew better than to push my luck." He swore as the file started to turn, then stopped and needed more coaxing and wiggling. "Do you understand how embarrassed I am that this is taking so long?"

"You're out of practice," she said gently. "You haven't done it in a long time."

And there was the forgiving, accepting purity in her voice that was like a drug to him. It made a pang resound in his chest.

"It doesn't change the fact that I'm doing it, Nina."

He was still a street punk deep down. A sex tape stud who had benefited from the very notoriety he'd resented. His profits had tripled while he'd been making headlines and, much as he'd felt cheapened by the scandal, he'd also capitalized on it. He'd fought to get the tape taken down, but there'd been a part of him that figured he deserved that grim chapter of his life because of the kind of person he was.

Nina's phone buzzed in her pocket. She glanced at it. "My sister. She'll want to know how things are going." She walked toward the door. "Do you want me to get a butter knife?"

"No." He wouldn't corrupt her any more than he already had.

Angela told Nina there was a photo of Nina and Reve gaining traction online. Back when she'd been living with Reve, they'd gone for dinner and had been caught behind a tourist taking a selfie. Now the grainy image was being blown up in every possible way.

"All the headlines are saying it's Oriel," Angela said with concern. "Even my clients are starting to talk about how much you look like her. I don't know how long I can pretend it's all a coincidence."

"I know. I'm sorry. This feels like a bomb going off in slow motion," Nina said, distressed at the thought of Reve being freshly linked to Oriel.

She didn't tell Angela what Reve was doing right now—or that Reve had basically broken up with her. Again. She finished the call and went into the bathroom to set a cool cloth over her eyes, trying to keep from tearing up with despair.

You want the kind of love you've always known.

She did. And she wanted that love *with him.* She was falling in love with him all over again—this time far more deeply because she knew him more intimately. He could throw his checkered past at her all he wanted, and it didn't change the fact that he'd been playing human shield since she had run into his penthouse ten days ago. He could say he was only betting on a horse with his investment in her work, but he had removed any obstacles between her and her long-held dream.

She *was* prepared to compromise those things she had always wanted because a greater want was taking its place inside her: Reve. She wanted Reve in her life.

I won't let you settle for less because we happen to be good in bed.

Was that all it was for him?

Did it matter what he felt? He'd been through a lot at the hands of others. He had told her no one had ever looked out for him. The last thing she wanted was to be as callous about consequences to him as everyone else seemed to have been. She knew he was trying to protect her from himself, but maybe she had to protect him from herself, too.

With gritty eyes and the deepest ache in her heart, she went back to the office and found him at the desk, files stacked before him. He had his laptop open and was using his phone to photograph documents. Drawers in the credenza were half-open.

Her heart leaped. "You got in?"

"Yes, but everything is in German."

"Oh. Of course." She moved to the sofa and dropped to sit, pretty much defeated by the weight of stress and problems surrounding her.

"I'm converting it to English through a translation app."

"Oh?" She perked up. "Have you learned anything?"

"That stolen evidence is not admissible in court—or so my lawyer tells me. He absolutely, positively advises I do not make copies of anything I have found on these premises without the express permission of the owners. I told him to draft a request for permission, which I will forward to them the minute I'm done here."

She gave a halfhearted laugh, struck by the sheer

absurdity of this situation, then asked, "Do you want help?"

"I've got a system going. But listen, from what I've read so far…" He turned another page, clicked his phone over it. He glanced at the image, tapped, then looked to his laptop, where he tapped a few keys. "I don't want to make any decisions for you that should be yours, but this has to be shared with the Dalal family. Your family got screwed, Nina. *You* did."

That wasn't news, yet her mouth began to tremble. "How?"

A click, a tap, a sharp glance.

"Take a minute to be sure. This will be difficult to hear."

"I need to know, Reve. Tell me."

Reve hesitated one more second, then tapped his laptop and read aloud, "'Female presenting at twenty weeks.' Lakshmi, when she first arrived," he clarified. "'Midwife suggests possible multiple pregnancy. Scan for confirmation declined.'"

"Declined by who?"

"Lakshmi's manager, Gouresh Bakshi. He was running interference." Reve tapped a few more keys. "She had sixteen weekly visits from the midwife, then, 'Twin girls delivered on either side of midnight. Maternal distress, a transfusion…' She doesn't regain consciousness for a couple of days. While she was out it says, 'Baby Monday placed as arranged.' You should see Lakshmi's signature on the documents." He ruffled through the pages. "I'm no expert, but it's a man's handwriting."

"Of course it is. She was unconscious! Is that really what they called us?" It was a good thing she was sitting down. She felt sick.

Reve's expression softened. "I'm afraid so." He tapped a file. "In this one, it says Baby Tuesday was placed with an American family. There's also a confirmation for a wire transfer for a revoltingly high payment with a note that labels it 'discretionary.' The banking info ties into the other payments from Bakshi for Lakshmi's care."

"Oh, my God." Nina buried her face in her hands.

"I know. Nina, I'm sorry." He rose and came to crouch before her, taking her cold hands.

"Who does something so awful to a woman who is so vulnerable and—"

"You were all vulnerable. He did that to all three of you."

"He just gave us away like p-puppies."

Reve shifted onto the couch and drew her into his lap. Nina should have been cried out, but these tears were different. They were for Lakshmi and Oriel and herself. She was breaking into agonized pieces as she imagined her birth mother awakening and learning her babies were gone, gone, gone.

"I feel so *robbed*."

"You were." He was rubbing her back, setting kisses on her hair. "You all were." He held her in strong, safe arms while she completely fell apart.

She wept until her eyes swelled shut and her whole body ached with grief.

* * *

"Nina."

Reve's raspy voice and the feel of his hand rubbing her arm dragged her awake.

She blinked eyes that felt like sandpaper and found herself in the den. Morning sunlight was beaming through the window. She had a blanket over her, a pillow tucked under her head.

"What—?"

"Farrah's making breakfast. There's a woman downstairs who wants to meet you."

"Oriel?" Her heart leaped into her mouth. She sat up so fast Reve had to lean back to avoid her forehead crashing into his unshaved chin.

"No. But I got a message from my doorman in Paris. Oriel came looking for you there."

Her head throbbed, and she couldn't hear anything but the blood in her ears. She was disoriented. Her heart was seesawing in her chest. She grasped at Reve's arm and he steadied her, but there was a stiffness to his touch, as though he was holding her off. The remoteness in his expression caused her unsteady heart to plummet into freefall.

Don't, she wanted to cry, as everything came rushing back to her. Still, she couldn't keep leaning on him. It wasn't fair to either of them.

She drew her hands into her lap and tried to catch up to what he was saying.

"How did she know—?"

"There's a photo of us online that people are saying is her. She must have tracked you to being with me."

"Oh, I forgot," she sighed. "Angela told me about that photo. I meant to tell you, but…" She looked to the credenza. All the drawers were safely closed, the tablecloth in place, and all the files were gone from the desk.

"I've booked a helicopter to take us to Paris as soon as we've eaten."

She noticed he was still wearing yesterday's clothes. "Have you slept?"

"No. Do you want come downstairs? This woman is married to the man who owns the café."

"Oh. Yes. Okay." She staggered down the hall to the master bedroom and made herself presentable.

When she came down, Reve was sipping a coffee at the windows. Farrah was gone and a woman of about fifty was on the sofa. There was a cup of coffee steaming on the table in front of her, but she had her hands clutched anxiously over her purse.

The air was so thick with tension it could have been sliced and fried.

The woman stood when Nina appeared. She searched Nina's face as Nina offered a faint smile. "Hello."

"I'm sorry to come here uninvited. I'm Inga Klein." She offered her hand. "Your, um…" She looked to Reve. "Your friend left his card with my husband yesterday and said you were staying here. My husband thought he was a reporter. I've just explained that my father-in-law has dementia. He doesn't have any information that would be helpful."

"I see." Nina looked to Reve, unsure if she should offer her real name. "I'm, um…"

"The other one," Inga said with a sad nod of wonder. "You're not Oriel Cuvier. I've been following her story very closely. As soon as my husband showed me the card last night, I knew you weren't her. You're the other one. Aren't you?"

"You know?" Nina felt Reve's hand take hold of her arm and ease her toward the sofa. Her knees felt like jelly.

"I didn't *know*." Inga sank back into her seat. "It was a suspicion that has haunted me for years." Her gaze pleaded for understanding. "I was fifteen when I got a job as a maid, cleaning cottages for the rich people being treated at the clinic. It was impressed upon me that I could never talk about anything I heard or saw."

Inga nervously clicked the clasp on her purse.

"I saw a lot of strange things. Eventually the Indian couple were just one more odd memory I locked away, but I've always wondered what happened to her. You look just like I remember her." She sent an unsteady smile, then looked down again, growing somber. "They claimed to be married, but they fought constantly. Not in English. I only guessed that it was about her pregnancy. She cried when he wasn't around."

She clicked open her purse and darted her hand into it, bringing out a folded sheet of paper with scorched edges. She offered it.

"She wrote letters and threw them into the fire when he got home. I don't know why I took this one. It has always tortured my conscience that I did, but once I had it, I couldn't bring myself to get rid of it. I think it's to your father."

Nina accepted it but was too upset to make head or tail of it.

"We can read it in a minute." Reve gave her shoulder a bolstering squeeze. "Is there anything else you can tell us?"

"Only that I came to work one day and he said she'd gone into labor the night before. He said I should pack their things because they would leave from the clinic as soon as she was discharged. He went out and I don't think he knew I was still there when he got back because I overheard him on the phone. He was speaking English and asked for Dr. Wagner. He asked if the woman who came in from the café had survived. Then he said, 'That's what we can do with the other one. Give it to her family. Tell them it was hers.' He said, 'Name your price.'"

Tears of remorse stood in Inga's eyes.

"I'm very sorry. My English wasn't very good. I thought I misunderstood. I was concerned about the mother, but no one connected to the clinic would tell me anything. When Oriel Cuvier began making headlines, I dug out the letter to see if there was a clue I'd missed. I've been trying to decide what to do with it. May I leave it with you?"

"Of course. Thank you," Nina said in a daze.

They thanked Inga and took her information, then Reve read the letter to Nina. The sentences were cut off by the burned sections of pages, but it sounded as though her biological father had had a son who was sick and Lakshmi had understood his need to be there for the boy.

"'…and when it's time he insists I must give it up…'" Reve continued. "She's referring to Bakshi, I imagine."

"'It…'" Nina repeated, latching on to the word. "Not *them*. She didn't know she was having twins."

"Doesn't sound like it. The last line is '…know what else to do. I wish you were here to…'"

"She sounds so tortured—and also as if she loved him." Her heart wrenched and twisted with bitter-sweet consolation. As she looked at the man *she* wanted and couldn't have, she knew exactly how her mother had felt. Torn, helpless and devastated.

Reve slept through the helicopter flight to Paris and only noticed how quiet and withdrawn Nina was as they drove into the city.

"Okay?" He tried to still the fingers she was liable to twist right off her hands.

"Hmm? Oh. Yes. You didn't have to come with me," she murmured. "This is when we said we would part ways," she reminded him with somber tension across her cheekbones. "I *need* to see her, Reve. I can't put it off any longer."

Her eyes said, *Even for you.*

"I know." He'd had a lot of time to think last night while she'd slept and he'd copied records. The more he realized what she was up against, the less he was able to leave her to it. He was confident the family of Lakshmi Dalal would pursue justice, but the only reason Oriel was so well protected was because her adoptive parents were wealthy and was married to a VP of TecSec. Reve would like to believe they would help Nina navigate all of this, but he didn't know that. He couldn't walk away until he was sure Nina would be safe.

"I want to meet her with you. See how she reacts."

"You know I'm too freaked-out to be brave, right?" She reached across and closed her clammy hand over his. "I know I should be saying I can do this alone, but…"

"I won't let you." He sandwiched her trembling fingers between his warm palms and directed the driver to Oriel's building. As they approached, they saw a throng of paparazzi lingering around the entrance.

"Looks like she's home," Reve said. "Do you want to go in? Or call her from my place?"

"In." She nodded convulsively.

They waited in the car while the driver went to the door.

As the driver rang the bell, the photographers began sniffing at the car's tinted windows, trying to see inside. A man in a dark suit appeared. A bodyguard, if Reve had to guess. He took Reve's card from the driver and glanced toward their car, nodding. He held the building's entrance door open while the driver came back.

Nina's hand tightened in Reve's right before the car door opened.

They stepped out and the paparazzi went wild.

CHAPTER ELEVEN

THE PHOTOGRAPHERS MUST have been baffled as to how Oriel had left the building without them knowing. Now she was with Reve?

Reve had glued her to his side with an arm that nearly cut off Nina's ability to breathe. He walked so fast her feet barely touched the ground, whisking her through the downpour of questions in French, Hindi and English.

"Oriel! Did you leave your husband? What is your relationship with Mr. Weston?"

Reve elbowed one of them who got too close, and then they were inside the building. The din faded as the bodyguard firmly shut the door and directed them up the stairs.

When Reve released her, Nina still couldn't breathe. She glanced at him in weak apology for putting him through the media storm and hurried up the stairs on shaking knees. The man who'd let them in brought her to a door guarded by another man. He knocked for her.

She blindly reached for Reve's hand. Her vision

was getting fuzzy around the edges. Her heart was all she heard as she waited. *Thump, thump, thump.*

The door opened.

The woman who stood on the other side was a version of herself that was more polished, a tiny bit taller, with a face that was a smidgen softer. If Reve's hand hadn't been crushing hers, Nina would have felt completely untethered to reality, as though she occupied two timelines and was committing the mortal sin of disrupting the space-time continuum.

Someone said something. Her ears were rushing with her hammering pulse. Her eyes were glossing and blinking in time with her reflection's. Her throat was dry, the air in her lungs growing thin. Weirdly, amid all that sensory confusion, the butterflies in her stomach settled into placid stillness, as though they were coming to rest after migrating across a continent.

It's been so long.

She didn't know if the voice was in her head or Oriel's as Oriel moved in the same split second Nina did. They stepped into a hug, and the most incredible sense of homecoming swamped her.

You're back, the voice in her head said. She was hugging a person she had no memory of knowing, but it was good and right and all she could think was, *I missed you.*

The piercing whistle of a teakettle startled the women apart.

Reve said, "You two sit down. I'll get that." He pressed them into the flat and closed the door.

He needed a minute. Reading about the cold and calculating way Nina had been separated from her mother and sister had filled him with outrage, yet he hadn't expected to feel this moved by her reunion with Oriel. He wanted Nina to be happy so it made sense that *seeing* her happy would please him, but this was exponentially more than that. His eyes were wet, and he didn't feel as though his sternum could withstand the pressure behind it as he went to silence the kettle.

He listened as he made coffee, though the women seemed too overcome to speak. They still hadn't spoken by the time he brought out two cups.

Oriel looked like a 3D copy of Nina. Like a wax figure in a museum. She was pregnant, he recalled, but it wasn't obvious.

Reve had the weirdest thought, though. This was how Nina would look if she was expecting—glowing with happiness.

A jagged truth tugged on his conscience. *You can't cheat her of that.*

"Do we need introductions?" Reve gave Nina's shoulder a squeeze to remind her he was here if she needed him. "I'm Reve. This is Nina."

"Oriel. Forgive me, I'm still in shock from learning about my birth mother. I had no idea I had a twin." She spoke in Nina's voice with a French accent, and Reve instantly liked her for it. Well, that and for the radiant smile she'd put on Nina's face.

"I'm sorry I wasn't here when you went to Reve's to find me," Nina said. "We were in Luxembourg, trying to find answers about…well, everything. I didn't actually know my parents weren't my birth parents. How could I have a secret twin?"

"Did you find anyone from the clinic?"

"No, but we found medical records on our delivery and…" Nina explained about Inga as she dug up the letter.

Oriel set her hand over her heart. "She kept it all this time?" She carefully unfolded the paper.

While Oriel read, Nina picked up Reve's hand from her shoulder and pressed her damp cheek to the back of his knuckles. It was a gesture of gratitude. Perhaps she was only trying to include him in her special moment. A few short months ago, he wouldn't have allowed himself to be drawn into anything this emotionally charged. As it was, he felt privileged to be part of this with her.

"This is so sad. My heart is absolutely broken for her," Oriel murmured, tears standing in her eyes.

"Mine, too." Nina then told her the rest, how Lakshmi hadn't been allowed to hold her babies or learn she'd had twins.

The sisters' anguish was palpable as they hugged it out, and Reve had to step away to a window and swallow back the lump that rose in his throat.

Behind him, they moved on to the deeper mystery of where they'd each gone after their birth, beginning to share and laugh in bemusement. Reve didn't listen to the words so much as the pleasing sound of Nina's voice in stereo. He didn't know how he was going to give her up, but his head was pounding with the knowledge that he had to. He cared for her more than he'd imagined he could care for anyone. It was a double-edged sword. The more he cared, the more he wanted to protect her from anyone who could harm her—himself included.

An abrupt knock cut off his rumination and the women's conversation.

Reve moved to open the door and confronted a man wearing the most hostile, contemptuous, death wish of a lip curl Reve had ever seen on anyone. Ever. And he'd seen a few in his lifetime.

"Ah," Reve said with false magnanimity. "The husband."

"Vijay!" Oriel leaped to her feet.

Nina rose and, even though she'd seen dozens of photos of Vijay Sahir with his wife, she was a little bowled over by how movie-star sexy he was. He crossed to kiss his wife's cheek.

Nina was envious of that, the simplicity of being in love and greeting each other with a kiss.

Oriel introduced Nina as her sister, and Vijay shook her hand graciously enough despite a notice-able hostility in his demeanor. He didn't shake hands with Reve.

"We don't know I'm her twin," Nina clarified, thinking he must be suspicious of her claim. "It's what the birth records we found would suggest, though."

"And anyone with eyes," Reve said laconically. She heard the edge of steel in his tone, as if he was offended Vijay might have doubts about her.

Had he forgotten that, as recently as yesterday, he'd been telling her what venal souls most people possessed? Vijay was allowed to be skeptical.

"I imagine Lakshmi's family has been inundated with people claiming to be her daughter. I'm happy to do a DNA test," she assured Vijay.

"Seems redundant, but I've already connected with our lab," Vijay said. "I'll arrange it shortly. I need to speak with my wife first." He looked at Oriel, and the air between them crackled with enough sexual tension that Nina immediately felt like an interloper.

"You should check in with your family, Nina. Warn them that things are about to get very chaotic," Reve said.

"Oh. Vijay will arrange protection for you." Oriel looked to her husband.

"Already in the works," he assured her.

"I can protect her," Reve said in a tone that sounded both offended and territorial.

"Do you think I'm going to let anything happen to my wife's sister?" Vijay moved aside with Reve to exchange cards.

"Shall we meet for dinner?" Nina invited, anxious not to lose another minute with her twin.

"Of course. I just need a few minutes…" Oriel sent Vijay a conflicted look, then put Nina's number into her phone and promised to text.

Minutes later, Vijay's bodyguard helped Nina and Reve slip out a side door and into their car undetected.

"I feel like we were rude, leaving so abruptly," Nina said, her head still spinning.

"Did you not see the way he was looking at me?" Reve's voice dripped with ironic amusement. "He blamed me for the photos that made it look like his wife was having an affair. I suspect that's why she came to Paris alone and was so surprised he turned up."

"Why would he be mad at you for that? It was my fault."

"He can't be mad at you. It would be like yelling at his wife while trying to apologize to her. He kicked us out so they could kiss and make up."

"Oh." They arrived at his building and darted in before any enterprising photographers caught them.

In the elevator, she asked curiously, "*Would* you have an affair with her?"

"I never sleep with married women," he dismissed firmly. "You?"

"Have I slept with a married woman? My sister. And my brother's cat preferred to sleep with me, which made him furious. Does that count as cheating?"

"Sure does. Home-wrecker."

They both laughed and his smile lingered. "You're happy. It looks good on you."

She was happy because she was still with him and they were bantering like the things they'd said yesterday hadn't happened.

As if they both suddenly recalled the conversation, they sobered. He stared at the doors, which conveniently opened.

"As I said at Oriel's, you should call your family,

tell them what to expect," he said as he let her into the penthouse.

Nina waited until he had shut the door to ask, "What *should* I expect? Are we saying goodbye for good now? It's okay if we are. I just—" she cleared the gathering thickness from her throat and almost dropped her phone as she drew it from her bag "—need to find a hotel."

"You're not going to a hotel," he said gruffly. "You still need my help, Nina. Tell your family you're safe and let them know I'll arrange security for them. I've already made preliminary calls. I'll have my people draft a statement, but we won't release it until we've coordinated with Oriel's people. Ask your family to sit tight for a little longer."

"How am I supposed to afford all that? Do *not* say you'll pay for it," she warned.

"I will pay for it. I protect what's important to me," he said implacably.

"Reve." She wanted to stamp her foot and also hug him with all her might. He was the most infuriating, endearing man she'd ever met. "I can't keep leaning on you. Not when—" The tendons in her throat flexed. "I don't want to lose your respect. Not after I've worked so hard to earn it."

"Bloody hell, Nina." He paced a few feet, then shoved his hand through his hair with uncharacteristic agitation. "You don't have anyone on your side. Not anyone who knows how to survive the mess you're in the way I do."

"I have Oriel." Was she being presumptuous? They

seemed to have an immediate connection, but maybe that perception was only on her side.

"You literally met her an hour ago. She has a husband and an unborn baby and her own family to protect. You can't be her top priority. Let *me* lead you through this."

"I can't do that to you, Reve." It killed her to say it, to provoke the darkness blooming in his expression as she rebuffed him. "It's everything you hate. You'll start to hate *me*."

"I can take care of myself," he dismissed with a wave of his hand. "It's you I worry about."

"And I'm worrying about you! Reve, what are we doing?" she cried, struck by the absurdity of it all. "We obviously care about one another. Why are we putting all these…things between us?"

"I'm simply trying to help a—" He cut himself off, his mouth tightening.

"What? Business partner? Is that what I am to you?"

Ironically, she had been terrified of this moment when she left the old Nina behind and became this new woman. Oriel's sister. Lakshmi's daughter. She hadn't known what to expect, only that her life would change. She would know more about herself and some of that would be difficult. It was.

But as she let go of her old self, and the layers of hurt and existential angst she had been using as self-protection, she saw herself more clearly than she ever had.

She was still Nina. She had loved Reve before and

she still did. Her love for him had been beating under her skin with her pulse all along, and she couldn't keep it in any longer.

"Reve, *I love you.*"

"Don't." He closed his eyes.

His rejection stung like a million ant bites. A wound opened in her chest, but she understood him so much better now.

"Don't say it? Or don't feel it? Because I can't control it."

"Don't feel it. I'm not worth your love," Reve said, each word scoring into her. "That's for people like your family. People who know how to love you back."

"It's okay if you don't love me back," she said. Her throat was tight with agony because, yes, deep down she longed for him to love her back. "I don't want you to say words you don't mean. You were right when you said I wouldn't want to marry and have children just to tick those boxes, but I'm realizing I would rather leave them unticked than give up the man I love."

He withdrew more firmly, his hands clenching into fists as though he was enduring some kind of intense pain.

"I won't force you to accept my love, either," she said with quiet dignity. "Love isn't supposed to be transactional. I'm not saying it to get something from you. I'm offering it freely. Here is my heart. Pick it up or not. That's your choice."

He still wasn't looking at her. The veins in his

arms stood out as he inhaled deeply and released a long breath.

"I am so afraid of hurting you again, Nina. Now I don't see how I can avoid it." His expression was anguished. Tortured. "I want to stay and protect you, but I don't want to lead you on. I don't want you to believe…" He pinched the bridge of his nose. "To think that I'm going to become more than I am."

A skip of hope pulsed through her.

"You're enough, Reve. You are. Could we…?" She stepped closer. "Could we agree to take it day by day and see how far we get?"

His expression contorted with conflict, but as she slowly approached, his arm shifted so his hand settled on her hip.

"This is why you're so damned dangerous to me," he said in voice thick with fatalism. "All I can think about is how I don't want to make you cry—"

She threw her arms around him.

Maybe I do love her, Reve thought as Nina sealed her mouth against his.

Whatever this feeling was, it was big and unwieldly. He was still trying to figure out how to grasp and hold on to it, and the trying made him feel clumsy and expansive and raw. He couldn't fudge something like that, though. His worst nightmare would be for her to look at him with disillusionment and betrayal again.

It made him take things very carefully as she led him to the bedroom. He undressed slowly, giving her time to be sure, before they slid naked into his bed. There he settled his mouth over hers with aching gentleness, trying to convey the need in him to protect her. Cherish her. Celebrate her.

When he looked into her eyes, he saw so many emotions he was certain he was physically falling through air. His throat thickened and his chest hurt. Every emotion filled him, then. Regrets and awe, conflicts and need, the heat of lust and the sweeter, softer glow that wanted her to know how incredibly precious she was to him.

A sting hit behind his closed eyelids. Joy. It burned his chest in a painful bliss as he swept his hands over her skin, wanting to gather and caress, worship and incite all of her.

She did the same to him and it was exquisite. She touched him with reverence even as she did all the things she knew drove him mad with pleasure. He couldn't help the broken groan that left his throat or the possessive growl that resounded in his chest.

He claimed every inch of her, too, caressing her with a delicate saw of his fingertip until she was shaking with need. Then he settled over her and slowly pressed into her, both of them sighing as they were finally where they needed to be. Together. One.

They stayed like that a long, long time, moving in small, savoring strokes, holding fast to each other until their bodies betrayed them and demanded more power, greater depth. They were basic elements then, creating heat and friction and, aligning perfectly, they melded into something new and gleaming and indelible.

Nina shivered and clenched beneath him. Reve's voice tore.

The waves of culmination soared over and through them, holding them at the brink of heaven for eternity, bathing them in its glorious light before slowly releasing them to drift gently back to earth.

With a sigh, Nina relaxed beneath him.

After a time, Reve gathered himself to withdraw, but she pressed him to stay inside her, whispering, "Not yet."

He shifted and they fell asleep still joined.

The next hours were a roller coaster of emotions, but Nina was at peace with it. She had Reve. Maybe they weren't committed for a lifetime, but they were united for now and that was enough.

Oriel and Vijay turned up looking like honeymooners. They could barely keep their hands off one another, which had Reve sending Nina a told-you-so look behind Oriel's back.

She bit back a smirk, then sobered when Vijay began rhyming off the security he was putting in place.

"That seems like a lot." Nina was daunted. "Is it really necessary?"

"Vijay is extra cautious. I'm afraid you've acquired more than a twin," Oriel teased. "You also get an overprotective brother."

"I already have one of those!" Nina said, pretending to be disgruntled before she added cheekily, "I guess there's no such thing as too many?"

"That's what I was thinking about sassy little sisters." Vijay winked as he stepped away to talk press releases with Reve. Nina grinned. She liked him.

Nina and Oriel sat to have their cheeks swabbed by a nurse who would personally courier their samples to a private lab. She said they would have the results by morning. "But, honestly?" the nurse continued. "This seems like a lot of money and trouble to state the obvious."

They were all thinking that even before Nina and Oriel discovered they were alike in ways beyond the physical. They laughed at the same things and disliked the same foods, and Oriel went into raptures when she saw the pop-up boutique Reve had installed in the spare room.

"Vijay," Oriel called from the doorway. "I'm throwing you over for Reve!"

"Reve already has one of you," Reve called back drily. "But I'm given to understand one can't have too many?"

Oriel snickered, then asked Nina, "How long have you two been together? I only ask because Vijay thought I had something going with Reve when your photo turned up." She began to comb through the racks. "I'm surprised there weren't more. Reve is very well-known in New York. We might have found each other sooner if I'd seen you with him."

"Reve hates the spotlight. He avoids photographers as much as possible." Nina didn't explain why.

Oriel's gaze flashed up and softened with compassion. "He won't enjoy the attention in India. I don't know how to prepare you."

After hearing the security measures, apprehension was sitting like heartburn in Nina's chest. She tried not to think of it and chatted fashion with Oriel, eventually showing her a couple of her own pieces from her luggage. Oriel gasped with delight.

"These are beautiful. You should make my maternity clothes." Then she joked, "We should start a label like those other twins who had a house here in Paris."

"The Sauveterres? Are you being serious? Because I'm so on board I'm riding all the way to the station."

"I was kidding, but…" Oriel cocked her head, considering. "Design isn't my strong suit. That would definitely be on you. I would excel at networking, though. I know a *lot* of people. Plus, I'm in India full-time. I could source textile and garment factories."

"I'd want it to be the fair wage kind," Nina said. "No exploitation."

"Agreed. Ethical from soil to shop. Prove to the industry it can be done. Are *you* being serious? Because I've been stressing about giving up modeling. I love this idea so much." Oriel excitedly locked her hand around Nina's wrist. "You're coming to Mumbai, yes? We'll hammer out our business plan while you're there."

Nina laughed at the idea of her dearest-held dream coming to fruition so easily—and with the perfect person.

She hadn't fully processed that she would go to

Mumbai, or that she had other blood relations besides Oriel, but one video chat with Lakshmi's brother, Uncle Jalil, and she longed to meet him. He already felt like family.

Jalil wept openly, deeply upset at the way his sister and her daughters had been treated. "Bring all the papers. I already have a lawyer working on this. Whatever settlement we win will go to Lakshmi's estate," he told them. "Oriel has been resisting accepting that, but you two are entitled to it. I want you to have it."

"I'm just happy to know where I came from," Nina told Oriel when they ended the call. "I don't want to offend him by refusing, but I really don't want her money."

"Same, but he's adamant. I suggested we use some of it to make a biopic on her life."

"Oh, I love that idea."

They sat down with the men then, eating grapes and cheese and crab croquettes while they finalized the press release.

"Do we bother waiting for the DNA results?" Vijay asked, glancing toward the terrace. "I think we're losing our chance to stay ahead of the story."

Photographers had been gathering outside in greater numbers since Oriel and Vijay had arrived.

Nina looked to Reve. It meant putting him under a microscope as well as herself.

"It's your decision." He squeezed her hand.

"It feels like the nuclear codes," she said with a pang, thinking it was the first test of this tentative future they had agreed to try. She glanced at Oriel.

"Do you want to run for shelter before all hell breaks loose?"

"Hell is already loose in my life," Oriel said wryly. "Honestly? I want to stand on that terrace and show the world I have a sister." Her eyes grew bright with happy tears, her smile wide and unsteady. "But you should do this however it suits you best." Her glance flickered to Reve as if she read Nina's concern there. "*I* know I have a sister. That's the most important part for me."

Nina knew then that she really did have a sister in Oriel. The truth was that she was equally excited to tell the world she had a twin.

Whether her sudden fame would destroy what she had with Reve was a question that could only be answered by letting the secret out. It wasn't a secret they could keep forever anyway.

She gave a jerky nod. "Let's do it."

CHAPTER TWELVE

NINA'S APPEARANCE ON the terrace last night with Oriel had set Paris on fire. The news traveled around the world within hours. Despite the downpour in Mumbai when they landed, even bigger crowds were gathered at the airport and outside the building where Oriel and Vijay lived. The roar when they paused to wave before hurrying out of the rain and into the high-rise rang in Nina's ears as they stepped into the elevator.

"It's a lot, I know," Oriel said with a small wince of empathy, leaning into Vijay.

"Settle in and rest," Vijay suggested, looping his arm around his wife. "Jalil and my sister will join us for dinner, but we'll put off talking about interviews and appearances until tomorrow or the next day."

"I think the baby needs to nap," Oriel said with a sleepy blink up at him.

"Then baby should." Vijay settled his hand on her belly, seeming completely enamored with her.

Nina's heart pinched and she glanced away, but her gaze was snagged by Reve's intense one. She looked down guiltily. She couldn't help it that she was envious, and wished he hadn't noticed. It put a lot of pressure on him that she didn't mean.

The pair stayed in the elevator while she and Reve departed two floors below her sister's penthouse into a very swanky apartment with a living space that opened onto a covered terrace overlooking the sea.

Nina immediately went to stand at the rail. Rain gusted toward them, but she only grinned at the storm waves and heavy gray skies.

"Doesn't it smell good?" She drank in the sweet, earthy, salt-scented air.

"It does, but—" Reve nodded at someone pointing a camera toward them from the beach twenty stories below. He drew her back into the apartment. "Can you imagine bringing a child into this sort of fishbowl?"

She bit the corner of her lip, debating how to react.

"Oriel's mother is a renowned opera singer so she's used to being the daughter of someone famous. She seems comfortable with the attention, but they weren't planning to have a baby this soon." In a private confidence between sisters, Oriel had confessed that she and Vijay had married because Oriel fell unexpectedly pregnant. Nina kept it to herself.

"Accidents happen," she said with a defensive shrug. "I'll try not to have any and certainly wouldn't deliberately let it happen, but you should probably consider that it could."

He walked into the kitchen and her heart sank. She followed and found him glowering. Her stomach cramped.

"Look, if you're not comfortable with that risk…"

She couldn't finish the sentence. She hated how tentative this was! Without any firm promises between them, every little thing felt as though it could defeat them.

"I don't like this kitchen. We need to remove that wall and put in an island so you can cook without me getting in your way."

"Really?" she said, perplexed.

"Am I being sexist? I thought you liked to cook."

"Sure, but that sounds very… I mean, I can't afford this place."

"The show has done well, and I have every confidence you and Oriel will quickly become a force to be reckoned with in the fashion industry. At some point, you absolutely will be able to afford this, but I'll buy it. That way we'll have somewhere to stay when we visit."

Her stomach swooped. "I thought we were taking this day by day. Did you hear what I just said about accidents?"

"Yes. And if I'm not comfortable with that risk, I can wear condoms as an extra precaution. I probably won't, unless you want me to."

"Really?" A bubble of optimism rose to press painfully behind her breastbone.

"Really. Let's go see if we like the bedroom."

The next days were challenging and busy, but Reve couldn't resent the demands and privacy difficulties when Nina was positively incandescent.

And while he still loathed the intrusion of paparazzi, he discovered what a disservice he'd done to her and himself in the past, when he had refused to meet her family. He had thought it would feel like an overstep to allow strangers into his personal life, but spending time with Nina while she got to know Oriel allowed him to see parts of her she had never revealed before. At night, she decompressed, confiding in him the complicated feelings she had about all of this. It formed tiny threads that meshed them closer together.

He enjoyed coaching her and Oriel on their business plan for the fashion house idea, too. Nina's confidence in her worth as an artist grew by the day, making him so proud he was in danger of becoming insufferable. Vijay's sister wanted in on their fashion label idea even though she was already busy with the security work she did with Vijay, and soon Reve was sent to do "boy things" with Vijay and Jalil. He enjoyed their company, too.

With the evidence Reve had found, Jalil was commencing formal legal action against Lakshmi's manager. Suing the clinic was much trickier since the business had been dissolved two decades ago and the doctor who'd colluded with Bakshi was dead. Still, they were going to try. In fact, Reve had just left Nina with Oriel and Jalil at the lawyer's office and was killing time by wandering down the block.

Restlessness chased him. He was ignoring his own business by lingering here with her, but he didn't want to leave, even though he knew she would be okay. Jalil was footing the bill on the legal proceedings and security. Everyone had welcomed Nina with open arms. She was regaining her sense of self and making decisions about her future. She didn't really need him.

Which wasn't as comforting a thought as it ought to be. If she didn't need him, why was he here? Because she loved him and he didn't want to hurt her by rejecting that love?

That was true, but he was also starting to realize that he needed her. He had already tasted life without her voice and touch and laughter. It was empty and meaningless if he didn't have their playful bickering or quiet moments of sincerity.

From the moment she had stumbled back into his life, he'd been thinking he should pry her out of it, and he hadn't once found the strength. He still didn't think he was right for her, but their soft promise of "wait and see" wasn't enough for him. He saw the commitment between Vijay and Oriel and knew Nina wanted that. Love, marriage, children… It still felt very foreign to him. Impossible to achieve.

Yet, every time he saw Vijay touch Oriel's belly, curiosity rose in him. He wanted to ask him, *What is that like? How does it feel? How do you know you'll be a good father*?

He looked at his ghostly reflection in a shop window and was struck by how much he looked like a younger version of his father. Had there been a time when that man had loved him, before he'd lost the woman he loved and gave himself up to a bottle of grief?

Could this man reflected back at him be a good father after that example had been set for him? Despite Reve's mind riffling through all the ways he would make a terrible parent, a resounding truth rose above the noise. Nina wouldn't let him fail. She would help him be better. *He knew that.*

A swell of possibility rose in him.

"Sir, would you like to come in? Can I show you one of those rings?"

Reve focused his gaze and realized he was standing outside a jewelry store.

"You still need to go to Berlin, don't you?" Nina asked Reve the next morning.

They'd had a late night. She and Oriel had been interviewed on a television show, which had been surreal, but seemed to result in a wave of public outrage for what had been done to Lakshmi and support for them. Reve had been quiet and distracted, and she wasn't sure if it was because of the attention or because he was growing tired of playing second fiddle to her needs.

"I have business in New York that needs to be addressed sooner than later. Why? How long were you thinking of staying here?"

"Forever?" she said on a wistful sigh and flopped onto the sofa. "I love it here, but I feel very far away from my family. I also haven't even started the work I need to do with Andre. I have to fill those orders so my investor doesn't send his goon squad after me." She reached her toe out to nudge him in the thigh.

"You're saying that having a twin isn't as convenient as it sounds?" He caught her ankle and sat to swing her feet into his lap. "Isn't it like having a clone? Can't you be in two places at once now?"

"Turns out, no. Family is many things, but convenient is rarely one of them." She shifted to straddle his lap, so in love with him she thought she might die of it. "Even so, you can never have too much."

She faltered slightly as she realized how that might sound.

"Nina, it's okay that you say what's on your mind and in your heart." He tucked her hair behind her ear and looked at her in a way that sent a spear of hope straight into her chest. "That's how I know I can trust you."

"Do you trust me? Because sometimes I worry it's not the publicity that will drive you away," she confessed softly. "I worry it's the moments when I get excited about Oriel's baby or I do something else that makes you think I need what she has. I only need you." She cupped his stubbled cheeks. "I promise you that."

"It seems impossible that I could ever be enough." He searched her eyes pensively. "I keep thinking that I need to do more."

When she started to shake her head, he tightened his hands on her hips, forestalling her from saying anything.

"I can't ask you to leave places where you have roots and family and people who love you to follow me around the world. Not unless I give you a good reason to."

She wanted to ask, *Such as...?* She had stopped breathing, and her eyes teared up.

Ask me to marry you, she silently pleaded, pulse rushing in her ears. If he was her family, she would go wherever he wanted to take her, convenient or not.

He swallowed and started to reach into his shirt pocket.

Her heart stuttered and soared with anticipation.

His phone rang in the opposite pocket. He swore, glanced at her sheepishly and made a face of annoyance as he drew it out and looked at the screen.

His features froze with concentration. Hardened. When he clicked it off, his expression was grave.

"I have to leave." He spoke quietly and with a finality that landed on her like a meteorite.

Her limbs became cold and unwieldly, too weak and heavy to fight him as he moved her off his lap and rose.

"Right *now*? Why? I'll go with you." Panic edged into her voice as she scrambled to her feet.

"No. Spend time with your family. Tell them..." His expression tightened. "Tell them I'm sorry."

Dread slid down her back in cold fingers. Nina scanned his features, growing more and more distressed. Maybe she and Reve hadn't made any promises for a future, but she had thought she would have more warning if he decided to leave.

"What happened?" She looked at the phone he'd tucked away.

"The smear campaign has begun."

"On *me*? By who? Lakshmi's manager?"

"On *me*. There's nothing Bakshi can say to discredit *you*, is there? You're an innocent victim. He'll only look worse if he comes after you. Better to say your accusations against him are being prompted by a man who lacks morals. One who makes up any story for money."

"Oh, Reve, no. I am *so* sorry." She took a faltering step toward him, but he was already putting up a hand to hold her off.

"It was bound to happen, Nina." He was speaking in a tone she hadn't heard in a long while, the one that said nothing could touch him. Except it could. She heard through that aloof tone to the pain it disguised. "He'll soon discover he has started a fight he doesn't want with a ruthless bastard who stops at nothing. But my past, and the dirty fight we'll have, cannot be your problem. So here we are. This time we really will end it."

"No." Pain began to seep like poison through her veins and arteries and nerve endings, growing too intense to bear. "Reve, I don't care what he says about you. I *love* who you are. Everything about you."

"Nina." His voice was gentle, as though he was holding something fragile and trying to release it into a breeze. "It's not just you I'm protecting." He nodded to the ceiling and Oriel and Vijay, two floors up. "They'll all suffer if I allow myself to be used as a weapon. If I leave, he has nothing against any of you. You don't need me anymore. You'll be fine."

"No, I won't! I do need you. We belong together. *You know that*. You were just about to ask me to marry you, weren't you?" she demanded, pushing the strained words through her tight throat.

He looked away and a muscle clenched in his jaw. "You don't want to be married to this. I've always known that, and you would have seen it, too, if you had really wanted to. When you do, you'll thank me for making the hard choice that you refused to."

"That's bull. You're being a coward."

His head jerked back as if she'd punched him.

"I'm doing what has to be done." He walked into the bedroom where he threw a few necessities into a bag, gave her one last look of agonized regret and then left.

She didn't go to the shower. She was too devastated for tears. She sat on the sofa in a paralysis of loss, unable to form a thought through the pulsing pain that enclosed her.

Eventually, she became aware that her jagged breaths were the only thing she could hear in the otherwise profound silence. She had never felt more abandoned in her life.

But she wasn't alone, she realized dimly, and ran in a blind hurry up to Oriel's apartment, banging urgently on the door.

"Nina? Are you okay?" Oriel let her in, alarmed.

"No! Something happened." The words stumbled against the sobs that were stacked like uneven blocks in her throat. "Gouresh Bakshi is dragging up Reve's past to discredit me and harm Jalil's case. Reve *left*. And I don't know how I'm going to bear it."

"Oh, Nina." Oriel's arms came around her.

Nina clung to her sister and heard Vijay swear vehemently.

"That can only mean one thing," he said.

He sounded so grim that Nina was pulled from her anguished need to weep and lifted her head. "What?"

"I'm next."

Reve's jet had gone back into service after dropping them here in Mumbai. It would meet him in Dubai, and a conventional executive jet had been chartered to get him there. He was stuck in a private lounge, waiting for it to make its way onto the tarmac.

Would he start drinking, he wondered? He tried not to use alcohol as a coping mechanism, but he really didn't know how he would survive leaving Nina. He had to protect her, though. Had to.

Because he loved her. He must. There was no other explanation for this feeling—it was as though a part of him had been amputated. He could hardly breathe.

Although he wanted to berate himself for letting it happen, he hadn't had much choice in the matter, either. Not from the first moment she had approached him at that New Year's Eve shindig, saying with the wide-eyed blink of an ingenue, *Your performance of boredom is extraordinary.*

He had never been bored again. Not while she was around. Now, all he could think was that his life would become a wasteland again. Meaningless.

Ironically, by leaving her, he was trying to be the

sort of man who deserved her. He was trying not to hurt her by hurting her. It was the most untenable position to be in, but he understood now. Love wasn't a selfish thing you used to make others do things. It was something that drove your own actions on another's behalf. It was complete selflessness. The sacrifice of your own happiness for their betterment.

Why was he forcing loss on her, though?

His phone pinged again. He'd been ignoring it. His PR people were becoming aware that his reputation was being attacked. They were reaching out for guidance and, furious as he was by Bakshi's efforts, another part of Reve couldn't care less. If he couldn't have Nina, what was the point in fighting? Let Bakshi do his worst. He'd rather be dead.

Someone was trying to video call. He gave in and pulled his phone from his pocket, but missed it. Vijay.

He wasn't in the mood for whatever rebukes Vijay wanted to spit at him. Reve's past was stinking up all of their lives, he knew that. That's why he was leaving—to mitigate the damage.

It bothered him that he was losing Vijay's respect, though. Friendships of any kind had always eluded him, but he and Vijay had fallen into a comfortable camaraderie. This whole experience of watching Nina meld with her sister's world had drawn Reve into believing he was part of that thing she was forming. The f-word. *Family.*

He wasn't meant to have such a thing, though. He was alone and always would be.

His phone was still faceup, so he saw the text from Vijay as it arrived.

You tool. Do you think you're the only one with dirt in his past? We're both under attack. If you care about Nina at all, you'll come back and fight with us.

"Sir?" A woman appeared beside him. "I can show you to your plane now."

"Why is this man intent on destroying my family?" Jalil lamented. He sat between Nina and Oriel, one of their hands in each of his. Vijay's sister, Kiran, was clattering away on her laptop, and Vijay was in the loft, issuing sharp orders in Hindi into his phone.

Jalil's lawyer continued issuing advice over video chat.

Nina shouldn't have tuned it out, but she was one raw, exposed nerve, throbbing with agony. Empty. It was all she could do to reassure Jalil that she didn't blame him for Reve leaving. It wasn't his fault that Gouresh Bakshi was lashing out.

The truth was that she and Reve had always been unsustainable. She had wanted to believe her love was strong enough to carry their relationship, but she realized that the mightiest bridge did nothing if the man she extended it to didn't trust it enough to come across. Although he could say he was leaving to protect her, deep down, he was protecting himself.

He trusted her, but not *enough*. And that destroyed

her. She didn't know how she would survive losing him this time, she really didn't.

Their discussions were disrupted by a sharp knock on the door.

They all went silent and looked at it.

Vijay came to the rail of the loft. "No one should be able to get up the elevator."

"Maybe it's—" Oriel glanced hesitantly at Nina.

"Should we guess? Or look?" Kiran rolled her wheelchair across the room and turned the latch. As she pulled the door open, she said, "It's about time you came back. Oh. You've brought a friend. Hello."

She rolled back far enough to let Reve in. He was accompanied by a blond, white man, tall and thin like a marathon runner, maybe in his early thirties.

Nina barely noticed the other man. She slapped her hand over a heart that had begun to pound. Her vision blurred as hot tears arrived in her eyes. *He came back.*

"Pascal Hansen," Reve said with a nod, his gaze not leaving hers. "He was arguing with the doorman in the lobby when I came though, trying to get them to call up and tell you he was here."

"I haven't had any luck with leaving messages," Pascal said, rubbing his hands on the seams of his jeans. "I, um—goodness!" He looked between Oriel and Nina. His bemused smile revealed a small over-bite very similar to Nina's.

She started to feel dizzy and clutched Jalil's hand even harder.

"I found a letter in my father's things when he passed five years ago," Pascal said. "I knew he'd had an affair when I was young and that I had a sister in India, but… I guess I have two?"

"You should get some rest," Reve said when he finally got Nina back to their apartment. She looked more emotionally drained and subdued than he'd ever seen her—which was saying something, considering she'd been riding one crisis after another for weeks.

He hoped the resolution they'd arrived at today would finally put the worst of that behind her. Through the afternoon and evening, everyone had been on calls with lawyers, putting pressure on Gouresh Bakshi from all sides.

Reve had spared nothing in his threats to sue the man into oblivion for defamation. Vijay had made similar threats. There was an element of bluff in both of them since they each had a muddy past, but the cost of defending himself was an expense Bakshi hadn't wanted to take on.

Pascal's letter from Lakshmi to his father had secured Bakshi's final surrender. Lakshmi had laid out everything—how the affair she'd had with Pascal's father, a Norwegian academic, had resulted in a pregnancy. How she'd been pressured into having the baby far from home and forced by Bakshi to give it up.

He said our baby would never be accepted because she was mixed race, so I chose a French couple who were also mixed race. I was told the wife was an accomplished singer and the husband a scholar, like you.

I didn't get to hold her or even see her. She was gone when I awoke. Perhaps that was for the best, because I don't think I could have released her if I'd held her.

I will hate him for the rest of my life, though. There doesn't seem any point in living if I don't have you or our child.

Once those sentiments were conveyed through the lawyers, word came back that Bakshi would make a settlement that included all the rights to Lakshmi's movies. It was a reclaiming of Lakshmi that meant more to all of them than any financial gain.

Pascal had a wife and children to get back to so he was returning to Norway, but he promised to bring his family to meet his half sisters very soon.

Nina called her family, and they were thrilled to hear she had a half brother and even more thrilled to hear that once this final announcement was made, things should finally calm down a little.

"Nina?" Reve followed her into the kitchen.

"I want some tea," she murmured.

"I can make it. Go sit down."

She set the kettle aside without filling it.

"How long are you back for?" she asked in a choked voice. "Because I can't keep doing this."

"Nina, I was trying to protect you."

"You're doing a terrible job!" she accused, flinging herself around to face him. "Life has run me over again and again and you haven't stopped any of it. You *can't*, Reve. Do you realize that? I mean, I don't want to sound ungrateful for all the things you've provided me." She sniffed and briefly covered her face as she gathered her composure. She lifted her face. "In some ways you've held off the speeding train while I untangled myself from the tracks. I'm grateful for that, but the only thing I have really wanted from you in all of this is *you*. Your presence next to me. And you *left*."

He pinched the bridge of his nose and moved out of the kitchen, but still feeling claustrophobic as he reached the dimly lit living room with the terrace doors blackened by night.

He saw Nina's reflection in the one and glanced over his shoulder to see her leaning her shoulder on the wall, arms crossed. The corners of her mouth were pulled down with despair.

"I was going to ask you to marry me," he admitted, and felt the sting of her flinch. "But how the hell does that go? *I love you, Nina. Here are all of my worst behaviors making headlines. Please marry that?*" he mocked.

"Okay. I will."

"Don't." He looked to the ceiling. "I will take you at your word, and I will lock you down for the rest of our lives because I cannot take being apart from you. Not again. Not ever."

"Okay." He sensed her coming toward him and felt her arms come around his waist, but kept his gaze on the ceiling, afraid she would see how wet his eyes were.

"Don't forgive me that easily. I know I was a jerk

for leaving. I was so…" His arms closed convulsively around her. "I was so *happy*, beginning to see a future with you. It felt too good to be true, and it was. Gone like a candle being blown out."

"*You* blew it out. You didn't trust *us*. It's not gone, Reve. It's right here."

"I don't know how to believe this will last, though."

"You just do. That's how this works. You trust my love is there and believe in it and feel it inside you. That's how I feel. I know you love me. I do."

He did let her see into his eyes then, wanting her to know that his love for her was so big inside him, he didn't know how to contain it.

She dragged in an emotive breath and set her hand against his face, her eyes filling with tears. "Oh, Reve."

"I love you, Nina. Will you marry me?"

"Yes," she said with a trembling smile.

He wanted to kiss her, but he couldn't see. He scraped the heel of his hand across his wet lashes, then patted his pocket and withdrew the ring. His heart hammered. He kept the ring in his closed fist a final second.

She closed her hands over his fist, keeping his fingers folded over it. "You know I only want a future with you, right? A ring isn't necessary." She kissed his knuckles.

"It is to me. I want the whole world to know we're committed to one another. There's a wedding band that goes with this, and I'll wear one, too. I picked it because it looked like it wouldn't catch when you're working. You can exchange it if you want to." He opened his hand and watched her closely.

"Oh, my God, Reve." Her eyes bulged, and she brought both hands to her mouth as she took in the square emerald set flat and framed by multiple diamonds adorning the wide band.

"You like it?"

"I *love* it, but…" She saw a shadow come into his eyes. "No 'but,'" she corrected gently. "I was going to say that you have to stop being so generous, but no. You're perfect exactly as you are. I love *you*."

Perfect seemed a stretch, but she placed her trembling fingers on his palm, allowing him to thread the ring onto her finger. It caused the most profound feeling within him, as if he was truly joining himself to her in a way that went beyond the physical, material world.

They were both blinking wet eyes as he brought her knuckles to his lips and kissed her hand. "Be mine always?"

"Always," she promised.

When he drew her close and kissed her, he felt the joyous light of her spill through him, filling him with all those hopes and dreams she had for them. It was thrilling. The possibilities before them were so endless he could hardly catch his breath.

They married in Albuquerque with her "American" family in attendance. While Oriel couldn't fly because she was nearing her due date, she was very understanding about not being included.

"It should be about you and Reve, not you and me," Oriel said, wryly acknowledging that they always became the center of attention when they went anywhere together. "Besides, my mother is planning a wedding reception for Vijay and me for next summer. You and I can celebrate each other's marriages then."

Any initial coolness over the way Reve had broken Nina's heart was quickly forgotten by her family when they saw how doting he was. Also, as a wedding present, Reve got her sister fast-tracked and financed for one of the top family planning clinics in the country.

When Angela tried to demure, he asked, "What's the point in having all this money if I can't do nice things for Nina and the people she cares about?"

"I see how confusing he is," Angela confided when she put the final touches on Nina's hair. "It feels like he's buying my good opinion, but also I'm a little bit in love with him for doing something so magnanimous."

It was as though Reve had never had people to spend money on before, and now he was determined to spoil rotten everyone close to her. Nina's father didn't know it yet, but Reve had paid off his mortgage. Her brother, the real estate agent, was also about to earn a stinking great commission from the house Reve intended to buy so they would have a home to stay in when they visited.

Nina's father walked her down the aisle. They were all very weepy for the people who couldn't be there, but when she arrived to place her hands in Reve's, her joy was absolute.

He nearly crushed her hands as he spoke his vows and gave the ring on his finger an extra push to secure it in place, ensuring she knew he was hers. Always.

They didn't honeymoon, both too busy with work, but they settled into the New York penthouse with a pleasant sense it was their primary home. Nina and Oriel were making progress on their plans to open a fashion house. Nina found the perfect studio space and was beginning to equip and staff it while coordinating production contacts in India with Oriel.

In fact, she was so busy, her husband was the one who noticed she'd forgotten something very important.

"Nina, do you know what day it is?" he asked, coming into the kitchen where she was making their morning coffee. He wore only his pajama pants.

"Tuesday."

"It's Wednesday, but I was looking for the eye drops and, according to this, you think it's Sunday." He held out the blister pack that she kept in the cabinet over the bathroom sink.

"No!" She snatched it from him and stared in horror. "I *always* remember."

"Except we wound up staying at the hotel on Saturday night after the gala and didn't come home until afternoon. Then you were up early Monday for that meeting, and Tuesday morning you were talking to Oriel while you got ready for work."

"I…" She wanted to say she would have noticed

this morning, but they'd had sex before rising and she had honestly completely forgotten. "I didn't do this on purpose."

"I know." He gave her a perplexed frown. "I just thought you should know."

"Okay, but if I miss this many, I'm supposed to throw the package away." She swallowed. "And we should use condoms for a few weeks until…"

The coffeemaker hissed behind her. She gave it a distracted look.

"Until we…um…" She swallowed again. "Until we know whether there's anything else to, um, worry about."

"I'm not worried."

"No, Reve. Do you realize what I'm saying? I'm not *protected*."

"Oh, my God, Nina. Yes. I know where babies come from." He chuckled. "Would you please stop having a panic attack?" He caught her hips to draw her close. "Honestly, this is a conversation I didn't know how to have, but ever since Angela said their surrogate was pregnant, I've been thinking about asking you when you want us to start a family."

"Oh." She pretty much melted into a puddle. "Short answer? From the day I met you." She stroked her fingertips along the fine hairs against his breastbone. "I've always known I wanted you to be the father of my children."

"Yeah?" His smile was a slow dawn of self-conscious pleasure. "Well, let's hope we just got lucky, then."

"Oh, I'm already lucky," she assured him, lifting her smiling mouth for his smiling kiss. "I'm the luckiest woman alive."

"And I'm the luckiest man. But just in case…" He tilted his head toward the bedroom. "Should we improve our odds?"

"Oh, yes. Absolutely we should do that."

They did.

EPILOGUE

Three years later...

"DADDY!" MARTI—SHORT for Marta, which was Nina's grandmother's name—came running at him the minute he entered Nina's studio above the showroom for the Lakshmi label.

Reve caught up his two-year-old and closed his eyes in a moment of deep gratitude as her small arms went tight around his neck, constricting his breathing and filling him with the most incredible sense of wealth.

"Look." She showed him her bandaged finger.

"Did you find one of Mommy's pins?" No matter how vigilant Nina was, here or at home, their daughter was a magnet for finding them. She never put them in her mouth, always bringing them to the nearest adult, but had pricked herself more than once.

"She found Mommy's scissors," Nina said, her expression appalled. She moved in a slow, heavily pregnant gait, cute as hell when she was all round like this. "I left them there—" She pointed to her worktable, well above what Marti could reach. "She pulled over that chair and stacked those books on it so she could reach. Because she heard me telling Auntie that we would have to cut the order off at ten thousand. So obviously, I needed the scissors."

"Mmm…helpful girl." He kissed Marti's cheek, proud even when he was daunted by what a resource-ful and determined little sprite they had created. "You're supposed to work at your own table when you visit the studio," he reminded, and set her in the cor-ner that was fenced in with a countertop over shelves where her baskets of toys and books were stored.

She couldn't crawl under it, but immediately stepped on the books she'd left stacked on the floor. She was over it and free in record time.

"That's what I'm up against when the nanny drops her off now," Nina said with a bemused chuckle. "I don't know whether to be proud or frustrated."

"I had the same dilemma when she turned off the power bar under my desk. IT loved me when I dragged them in and that's all it turned out to be."

"No one in the history of having children said it was easy," she said with a rueful shake of her head. She absently moved his hand on her belly so he could feel their second baby moving. "I wouldn't have it any other way, though. This is exactly the life I wanted. Messy and confusing and so full of love I can hardly stand it. Thank you." She looked up at him with the smile that wrapped him up in so much love, his heart could hardly bear the force of it. His knees went weak.

"It's the life I didn't know I *could* have. Thank

you." He loved her back with everything in him and bent his head to kiss her, wanting her to know it, but he kept one eye on—

Marti bent and immediately came toddling over. "Here, Mommy." She held up a pin.

"Ah. Thank you, baby. Should we go home with Daddy?"

Marti nodded and held up her arms to Reve.

Home. Reve loved that word. They had several, but whichever abode they were in was home so long as he was with his family.

And three weeks later, when he returned to the penthouse with Nina and their son, it was even better.

* * * * *

WE HOPE YOU ENJOYED
THIS BOOK FROM

HARLEQUIN
PRESENTS

Escape to exotic locations where passion knows no bounds.

Welcome to the glamorous lives of royals and billionaires, where passion knows no bounds. Be swept into a world of luxury, wealth and exotic locations.

8 NEW BOOKS AVAILABLE EVERY MONTH!

HPHALO2021

HPCNMRA0921

#3949 PROOF OF THEIR ONE HOT NIGHT
The Infamous Cabrera Brothers
by Emmy Grayson

One soul-stirring night with notorious tycoon Alejandro leaves
Calandra pregnant. She plans to raise the baby alone. He's
determined to prove he's parent material—and tempt her into
another smoldering encounter...

#3950 HOW TO TEMPT THE OFF-LIMITS
BILLIONAIRE
South Africa's Scandalous Billionaires
by Joss Wood

On a mission to acquire Roisin's South African vineyard, tycoon
Muzi knows he needs to keep his eyes on the business deal, not
his best friend's sister. Only, their forbidden temptation leads to
even more forbidden nights...

#3951 THE ITALIAN'S BRIDE ON PAPER
by Kim Lawrence

When arrogant billionaire Samuele arrives at her door announcing
his claim to her nephew, he sends Maya's senses into overdrive...
She refuses to leave the baby's side, so he demands more—her as
his convenient wife!

#3952 REDEEMED BY HIS NEW YORK CINDERELLA
by Jadesola James

Kitty will do anything for the foundation inspired by her tumultuous
childhood. Even agree to a fake relationship to help Laurence, the
impossibly guarded man from her past, land his next deal. Only,
their chemistry is anything but make-believe!

"I'll speak plainly." The way he should have in the beginning, before she had him ruminating.

"All right."

"I'm close to signing the man you met. Giles Mueller. He's the owner of the Mueller Racetrack."

She nodded.

"You know it?"

"It's out on Long Island. I attended an event close to it once."

He grunted. "The woman you filled in for on Friday is—was—my set date for several events over the next month. Since Giles already thinks you're her, I'd like you to step in. In exchange, I'll make a handsome donation to your charity—"

"Foundation."

"Whatever you like."

There was silence between them for a moment, and Katherine looked at him again. It made him uncomfortable at once. He knew she couldn't see into his mind, but there was something very perceptive about that look. She said nothing, and he continued talking to cover the silence.

"You see, Katherine, I owe you a debt." Laurence's voice was dry. "You saved my life, and in turn I'll save your business."

She snorted. "What makes you think my business needs saving?"

Laurence laughed incredulously. "You're a one-person operation. You don't even have an office. Your website is one of those ghastly pay-by-the-month templates. You live in a boardinghouse—"

"I don't need an office," Katherine said proudly. "I meet clients in restaurants and coffee shops. An office is an old-fashioned and frankly completely unneeded expense. I'm not looking to make money off this, Laurence. I want to help people. Not everyone is like you."

Laurence chose not to pursue the insult; what mattered was getting Katherine to sign. "As you like," he said dismissively, then reached for his phone. "My driver has the paperwork waiting in the car. I'll have him bring it around now—"

"No."

It took a moment for the word to register. "Excuse me?"

Katherine did not repeat herself, but she did shake her head. "It's a kind offer, Laurence," she said firmly, "but the thought of playing your girlfriend is at least as absurd as your lie was."

Laurence realized after several seconds had passed that he was gaping, and he closed his mouth rapidly. He'd anticipated many different counteroffers—all that had been provided for in the partnership proposal that was ready for her to sign—but a refusal was something he was wholly unprepared for.

"You're saying no?" he said, to clarify.

She nodded.

"Why the hell would you say no?" The question came out far more harshly than he would have liked, but he was genuinely shocked. "You have everything to gain."

Don't miss
Redeemed by His New York Cinderella,
available October 2021 wherever
Harlequin Presents books and ebooks are sold.

Harlequin.com

HPEXP0921